Elisabeth Reichart

# FEBRUARY SHADOWS

Translated from the German *Februarschatten*

First Printing
Verlag der Österreichischen Staatsdruckerei
Vienna, 1984
ISBN: 3-206-000005-X

Reissued by Aufbau Verlag, Berlin, 1985

Afterword by Christa Wolf printed with permission of the author.

Cover design: Georg Eisler, Vienna

Elisabeth Reichart

# FEBRUARY SHADOWS

Translated and with Commentary by
Donna L. Hoffmeister

Afterword by
Christa Wolf

Ariadne Press
270 Goins Court
Riverside, California 92507

# 1

The telephone rang at night. The daughter, who was stay-ing with her then, got up. Hilde went out to the staircase. Sent the daughter back to her room.

To hear this word-that is my responsibility.

Hilde observed herself. How she went down the stairs. Laid her right hand on the phone. White skin. Deep wrinkles. Deeper than usual. How this hand clutched the receiver. Picked up the receiver. Brought the receiver closer.

She had listened motionless to the quiet voice of the nurse on night duty. A voice that did not sound impatient even when it had to ask again and again: Are you still there. This matter-of-fact composure.

This quiet voice had nothing to do with that word. That word would have called for screaming and raging. In order to be absorbed!

They had found him in front of the wash basin. Dead.

Anton is dead.

Hilde only needed to nod her head in order for Erika to cry. Touched her mother. Hilde pushed the daughter away: "Leave me alone."

The eyes of your daughter which had cried themselves out. The GUILTY eyes of your wife. - Anton, I know I am GUILTY.

I left you ALONE. ALL ALONE. Just as I left Hannes alone. My brother!

My ONLY brother. Among all my brothers. No matter how many brothers I had.

I abandoned my brother. Just as I did you.

You lay alone in your room.

Hannes hung alone from the pear tree.

You got up alone.

Hannes got up too. Earlier.

Went to the wash basin.

Thirst!

Collapsed in front of the wash basin.

You couldn't reach the bell. Hannes couldn't reach anyone.

You'll never get up again.

Just as Hannes didn't get up. Hannes, whom they led to the tree. Those who were led.

Hannes wasn't one of them.

No one led Hannes.

I am GUILTY.

I LEFT you ALONE. I went away from Hannes. That began long ago, so long ago. You were afraid of BEING ALONE.

Your room was cold. Was white. That February-morning was also white, white and cold

when Hannes hung from the tree

on which he died. Died alone.

GUILTY then. GUILTY today.

They will think today, what they thought then:

That it would have been better, if I had died.

No tears.

Wanting to scream.

Only wanting to scream one word: No!

Not being able to scream. The quiet voice on the telephone had determined the tone in which she would speak about it from now on. The circumlocutions are nothing new. An often repeated occurrence.

All the GUILT has been in me for a long time. Has been in the shadows. Which now make the darkness distinguishable.

Tree-shadows, people-shadows, sound-shadows. They disintegrate me.

Life has been taken away. You have been taken away.

No! Not Anton! Take me. Don't you hear! Take me.

But not Anton!

Not Anton.

No. Wait.

You have to give me a few days time. Only a few days. I have to take care of Anton's funeral.

Then you can take me.

Then.

Me.

Anton deserved a proper burial. He should have a nice burial. Not like that of Hannes. That wasn't a burial. That was like running the gauntlet. She didn't want to have to experience that again.

Hilde got up. Looked for Anton's key to the wine cellar. Did not find the key. Took the axe. Broke the door open with it. That door which had been locked for so long.

But not even the wine could drive away the shadows - she hadn't counted on that. And she hadn't anticipated that the GUILT would not decrease but would just become hazy. She couldn't fall asleep, until the shadows had become her truth; until they let her be. Not until Hilde lost her fear that the shadows were perhaps just hiding. Instead of going back into the wall. Into this very old, very strong wall. Only it was able to hold these shadows for a while. She already heard the men who worked the early shifts driving away. Or coming home. The neighbor coughed his morning cough. The neighborhood women made coffee for their men.

Hours later the question: why try to wake up.

Maybe I should give in to my tiredness. After all I have always given in. But then I would be just like that old woman. Who has been asleep for months. Who has to be awakened in order to eat. Who falls asleep during her meal. Sleeps. No. I don't want to be like that old woman. Why does she live. Lives asleep. I can't stand her any longer. I never want to see her again.

Once Hilde said that to Erika. That she hated the old woman. The old woman who is allowed to live asleep. While her son had had to die. But once again the daughter let her down. Didn't want to understand the mother. Said things that shouldn't be said. Erika told her that the grandmother was tracing her memories back further and further. Was living memories. Was going back to her beginning. And the beginning would be the end. Hilde had turned away. Away from the daughter. Away from the old woman. Back to her hatred.

Erika thinks only about the old woman. She never thinks about me.

And it is I who really NEED her.

But Erika doesn't notice that.

She lets me down. DESERTS me.

Everyone has DESERTED me.

Why get out of bed. So DESERTED. And not being able to forget BEING DESERTED. Like the other time. The time before you were there. It was cold. It was night. A February-night. Then I was still able to forget. I forgot that February-night. But you, you I must not forget.

The others have forgotten Anton already. She had to admonish the daughter on her visits to go to Anton's grave. Whereas I go to your grave every day. Always the same thing. Center of life. Something to hold on to. New every day.

Countless women go with her. Many in perpetual black. Even she had worn black for one whole year. But then she laid aside the external mourning. Some days she goes down the path to the cemetery several times. Goes so often that no blade of grass remains on Anton's grave. Until the grave caves in. Anton's grave. Then again she is able to go back to his grave only after several weeks have passed. Had let others tend to it in the meanwhile. Or the awkward hands of the daughter. Then this grave was no longer her grave.

Then she began to dance. Danced her cares away. Her futile cares. Danced the parson away who wanted to drive her out of the cemetery. She, who from the beginning had been at home in cemeteries. Danced the blades of grass away. The large blades of grass that had always annoyed her. Danced.

To know the one anxiety. The anxiety of being different, of being EXCLUDED. As in the past. Too often. No. Only once. When the teacher sent me into the corner.

When she only had the corner to herself and the laughter of the other children at her back. And later, later she also had wet herself. The wetness between her legs. Which was warm at first. But only a short while. Until it reached the floor and Hilde stood in a puddle. Until the puddle was seen by the teacher. The laughter became louder.

Hilde ran away. Just to get away. Ran.

I never want to belong again to those who are EXPELLED.

No matter what happens.

I want to belong to everyone.

To everyone of the others.

Now I am different again. Now I am again one who could have been EXCLUDED.

Without Anton you are nobody. She had had to hear that often during her time with him. Her sister-in-law had emphasized it at every opportunity. Had emphasized it loudly. So that it sounded like the laughter of the school kids behind her back. Standing again in the corner. Running away again. Only now she knew where to run to. Ran home. Ran to Anton.

I can't run to you any more. But into the house, which you and I built. Into this house I'll always be able to run.

No one can take this house away from me.

Why should they EXCLUDE me. They have no reason. No reason? It is a laughing matter actually. They don't need reasons. They have never needed reasons. And every reason would have been as bad as no reason.

Those are certainly not my ideas. Those are Erika's ideas. Erika has an easier time of it. She doesn't have my fears. Fears of being EXCLUDED. At most Erika excluded herself. With this demonstration against atomic war.

As if any of us could do something to prevent war.

Hannes? — Yes, Hannes tried. But even Hannes wasn't able to do anything. He remained alone. All alone. And soon Erika will also be alone. Like Hannes. In February. If she doesn't stop talking about her fears. About the skeletons. Which she sees faintly glimmering in her sleep. Then she will experience being laughed at. All the laughter, all the fears will gather around her. Will rule over her.

Erika has not yet experienced how important accusations can become. So important that they penetrate into me. The accusation of my sister-in-law: "You are nothing without Anton! Nothing! You would never have come to anything without him!" And how such alien accusations become one's own questions. — What am I without you? How everything sticks together and there is no way to dissolve it. None.

My sister-in-law soon had it easy. Soon her next accusation seemed credible. That I had her to thank for my marriage to you. That I should thank her for it. Every time she talks about it. She talks about it a lot. I have to make myself small. Very small. In order not to be EXCLUDED from the circle of the grateful. These nets after a decision. Are there decisions made too early?

At the same time I know that her claims are wrong. My being introduced to you was not enough, could not have been enough for us to marry. At one of the many Nazi victory celebrations during the war. You were standing next to your sister-in-law. I went up to the two of you. No. Up to you alone. You said your name. I said my name. Then the victors came up to you. Then the victors exchanged names. There were only victors.

The first thing Hilde noticed about Anton was his voice. His quiet voice. Among all the voices of the victors. It was hard to modulate one's own voice to his voice. A man who spoke so softly. Who did not like loud words. Hilde had only ever heard loud words.

I practiced speaking softly.

You had enough troubles. My voice should not be an extra problem for you.

No. You didn't deserve this trouble too.

Just as I didn't deserve being EXCLUDED. Mrs. Roth visits me. Whenever she needs something. And she visits me every Monday evening. To watch the television series. At home her husband watches the sports. I can visit Anna only during the day. When her husband is at work. I was also allowed to visit her in the evening when I was with you.

Everything was different with you.

Erika? Erika visits me more often than she used to. But Erika doesn't count.

What else? Nothing.

No invitations. No visitors.

The separation doesn't just apply to you. It applies to many people.

I can't stand this apartment. This empty apartment. I'll go for a walk. As I used to do with you. Slowly so that you don't overexert yourself. Only a short walk. Yes. I'll go for a short, slow walk with you.

Just before Hilde came back to the housing project she noticed a cat beside her. The cat stayed with her. Waited until Hilde unlocked the door. Went with her into the house. A black cat.

Where do black cats come from.

She had had a black cat once before.

Never wanted a black cat again.

The first black cat had also run under her feet. It ran beside her for a few days as she came home from school. Finally Hilde had taken it home with her in her school bag. Took it secretly into the upper room. Laid it in her bed.

Saved it something to eat from her own dinner every day. A difficult procedure. So many eyes. Which were waiting until no one wanted anything more to eat. Hilde shared her bed with her sister Monika. Monika promised not to betray her secret to their parents. When Hilde brushed her hair at night. Until she fell asleep.

This brushing her hair so long.

This cursing to myself.

This desire for a completely different movement of my hand.

But the black cat was there.

Once Hilde came home later than usual because of an air raid alert.

The black cat was dead.

But when Erika had found the black cat, the war had long been ended.

Always black cats.

After the air raid alert Hilde's father was waiting for her. Waited for her outside the front door. With the fly swatter in his hand. Hilde sees him standing there when she came to the large nut tree. Thinks she can smell the alcohol on his breathe. Anticipates that he is waiting for her. Not for any of his other children. She goes up to him slowly. Sees the neighbors waiting at their windows for the great spectacle. Sees the intent eyes of Pesendorfer. Goes on.- Where should I have run to.-

Hardly even feels the rubber fly swatter. Only hears the drunken voice of her father: "I wrung the neck of that beast.

Snap.

That was the end of it."

But I didn't wring the neck of the daughter's black cat. I only wanted to force Erika to take the cat away. Away. Far away. I only did that because the cat was so dirty. Because it was much too dangerous for the child to keep. Because she cuddled up to it so.

With this cat there was no crunching.

The crunching that I still hear had to do with my first and ONLY cat.

Later there was only the crying and pleading of the daughter. But I remained firm.

Hilde sees the father become relentlessly larger. Sees herself become smaller. Like the cat, just as small. Sees herself creep away from the father. Just as the cat had perhaps tried to creep away. Hears him speaking drunkenly behind her. That there is no money for such nonsense. Almost chokes on his stammering. That had taken her cat away from her.

But I didn't take anything away from the daughter.

No one took anything away from the daughter.

It was just from me that they were all able to take something away.

The daughter was allowed to keep the cat after all. Erika hid herself with the cat. Until Anton had come home.

Persuaded you, as I had never been able to persuade you.
Simply pushed me aside. You enjoyed her pleas. Ex-
plained that it was better for an only child to grow up with
a pet. When I saw your hand stroke our daughter's head,
I was no longer able to tell you about my own cat. Not
even about the easy time our daughter has. Much too
easy. And what a difficult time I had had in comparison.
-Much more difficult even now.

In order not to be EXCLUDED from the caressing hands,
she agreed. She knew for herself however that she would
remain firm.

Neither Anton nor the daughter had taken the neighbors
into account. They were upset about the noise the cat
made at night. Complained when there were holes in the
new beds of their garden.

One night I drowned the daughter's cat. Because of the
neighbors.

Anton agreed to it. Didn't accompany her on her ride
through the dark housing project though. Down to the
river.

At first she wanted to throw the cat down from the bridge.
When she took the sack out of her handbag, she heard
people coming closer. Had quickly left the bridge. Had
pushed her bike further onto the river bank. Had been
afraid. Had taken the bushes to be people. This way at
least she hadn't had to think about the cat. About the black
cat. Which she looked at for a few seconds. Seconds
during which she cursed the daughter and him. Because
it wouldn't have been necessary. That she stood here,

froze and trembled. That the cat looked at her so. As she didn't want to be looked at. If the two of them could only have listened to her for once. Do it quickly. Without thinking about it. Now. Since the decision had been made. Had been made for a long time.

There was no snapping. There was no crunching to be heard. There was a dull sound. When the sack fell into the water.

She hurried back to the street pushing the bike. Got caught on a willow. Fell down. Cut open her hand. Felt ill. Looking at her blood.

Fear kept her going to the street. There she let her bike fall into the ditch. Began to vomit. Vomited all the cats and all the cat memories out of her.

She told the daughter that she had brought the cat to a farmer.

The daughter cried.

No black cats anymore.

Years later she gave herself away.

She didn't notice right away. Only when she looked at the daughter by chance, who sat across from her with her white face and who looked through her with eyes taken back, whom she could not reach for a long time, only then did she notice her mistake.

When Erika looked at her again, it was as if she looked at a stranger. Hilde looked away.

The door bell rang. Hilde hesitated. It rang again. She went to the window. Pulled the curtain carefully aside. Looked out. Mr. Funk from the housing project was waiting in front of the door. Does the cat belong to him? She didn't dare behave as if the cat was not in her apartment. The neighbors saw everything.

Mr. Funk did not ask about the cat. He asked to come in. He wanted to talk to her about the Retirees Union. Since her husband had been a member of the Austrian Socialist Party, it was a matter of course that he concern himself with her after her period of mourning. Even though she had unfortunately never been a party member. That might still happen. Mr. Funk smiled. Hilde did not smile back.

So they still know.

How often did I tell you: quit the party. Immediately after we didn't get the apartment they promised to us, you should have quit.

But no. You could be as obstinate as your daughter.

And now here I am.

What is Mr. Funk saying?

That the Retirees Union has nothing to do with politics. Only with leisure activities. Outings were arranged. There were inexpensive vacation opportunities.

She would get to know a lot of nice people. Evening gatherings once a week.

What will the neighbors say if I don't join!

. . . All retired persons in the housing project were members of the union. . . I would most certainly stick out if I am the only one to stay away.

Maybe the neighbors would think I consider myself to be too good for them.

No. I must not provoke that. She signed the membership card. Let herself be congratulated about the well-considered decision. Took an events calender in her hand. Promised to come to the next evening gathering.

Had she done the right thing? Anton never went to a gathering of the Austrian Socialist Party. Except while they were waiting in vain for a new apartment. He had paid his dues a year in advance. Had kept the dues collector waiting in the hall. Had sent Hilde after the money. Had prevented every conversation with the absent-minded expression on his face.

She had almost convinced him to quit the Austrian Socialist Party. Meanwhile no one was interested anymore in the kind of past one had. When the past pushed itself again into the present through the questions of their daughter. Having forgotten everything to no avail. The father's brow wrinkled to no avail. The years harmless to no avail. Their daughter's questions crept in between the wrinkles and the innocent things. Erika's questions.

After her first question: "What party did you belong to during the period of National Socialism?" Anton had pointed to Hilde and said: "Your mother was still a child. What kind of a question is that!" Had kept himself out of it. Erika could not be appeased without an answer. Soon she gave up with Hilde. But she kept asking the father. Then he tried to get the upper hand by speaking of his membership in the Austrian Socialist Party. But it was of no use. Their positions only became more entrenched. Hilde remembers one sentence. One of Anton's sentences. One which she had not expected: "If I had been a Nazi, I would not have been admitted into the Austrian Socialist Party after 1945."

That was the only time that the daughter had laughed at the father. Anton sat helplessly across from his daughter. He should never have permitted it to come to this. That a daughter should laugh at a father. Even if his daughter's laughter sounded sad. Even if his daughter noticed that he was talking nonsense. Even if his daughter knew of his unfulfilled expectations. Or precisely for that reason.

How could she laugh so lightly about expectations. When in her case they were always fulfilled. Erika wanted to be important like Anton. And she was too for herself and for Anton. Erika wanted to LEARN also. Was allowed to

LEARN the things Anton had had to teach himself tediously long into the night. Erika just had no idea. How that was.

In earlier times: only that person was allowed to LEARN who had connections to the party, only that person was significant who took part. Yes. Took part. Hilde heard Erika's question: Took part in everything? And heard how the daughter held the grandmother up to her. She had told Erika how the Nazis came to take her son away. Right after the occupation. She threw the Nazis out. They never came back. They never needed to come back. When Anton told his stepfather about it, he joined the Storm Troopers. He took Anton to Hitler's Youth Organization.

From that day on the grandmother had not spoken another word to her second husband. Up until he died. Then she said one sentence to him. Only a single sentence: "If there is a God, he will forgive you as little as I have forgiven you."

In her memories Hilde heard Anton shouting. Heard the daughter shouting. She felt COLD. These loud voices. She knew them. She had had to live in such loud surroundings for twenty years. Now she no longer wanted to hear such shouting. Now that she had finally learned how to speak quietly. Had learned it on Anton's account. Had learned it for him. For her Anton. Whom she had never heard shout before.

She heard Anton's threats against Erika. Heard Erika's attacks against Anton. Both were stubborn. Anton would not talk about the past. Erika wanted to hear about nothing else.

Wanted to hear Anton's story in every story. Would not be kept from it.

I know the daughter. No one knows the daughter as well as I do.

She has been like that since she was a child.

She had lain on the floor. Had kicked. Had screamed. On account of every petty thing. Sometimes Hilde had stuck the daughter's head in a pail of water. In order to bring her back to her senses. Because spanking her didn't help. Besides Hilde didn't like to spank. Only sometimes. With a wooden spoon. Never again with her hand. Anton had forbidden her to do so. He didn't want to see the imprint of her fingers. After all Erika was a girl despite everything. Even though he had wanted a son. When Hilde took her hands away from the daughter's head, when the daughter stood wet in front of her, this child looked at her as if it hated its mother. Only then did this child take time to breathe. Hilde had begun to fear this expression on her face. Had gradually given up fighting against their daughter. Never wanted to look into such a face again.

Their daughter would not let any questions go unanswered. At some time or another the shouting had stopped.

Had Erika actually succeeded in finding her way to Anton?

For after their shouting his reactions were different. He didn't threaten to do away with her allowance. He didn't throw her out as he had often planned to do while lying beside Hilde in bed. He took an even greater interest in her.

Anticipated her visits as never before.

They talked to one another for hours.

EXCLUDED me once again.

Neither of them paid attention when Hilde wanted them to stop. Anton came to bed only when it was very late in the evening. But even there the daughter took Anton away from her. During such nights he never took Hilde's hand. His body never touched hers. Once she tried to take part in the discussions. Didn't want to remain OUTSIDE. He had become paler because of one sentence of hers. He said with a dismissing voice: "It was not so simple as that. You don't need to try to fool us. Nor yourself."

Then she was never able to try again.

Withdrew with her magazines. Or turned on the television.

Both of them remained sitting in the kitchen. Never joined her.

Those were not very pleasurable evenings in front of the television. There was no family life any more.

That was something which should not have been.

Hilde was no longer able to be angry even with the daughter about the rifts she had caused between Anton and herself. Had forgotten in the past year how to be furious. Was sad when Erika did not say on the telephone that she would come by on the weekend. Was sad during visits. Erika would DESERT her again after all in a few days. And while Erika was with her she did not know where all her expectations had vanished to. Did not know anymore what she had wanted to tell Erika.

These rare visits. Since Anton's death they were more frequent.

Does Erika come more often on my account or because of the novel which she is writing about me?

Does Erika ask so many questions about the past because she is interested in me or because she needs answers for her book? Surely it was only on account of the book.

It couldn't be because of me.

Erika was never interested in me. Only in you. You were important to her. You didn't want to talk much at first either. But Erika made an effort with you. On the other hand, she hardly asked me anything. She is concerned about me only now that she is writing this book. A book about my life.

What is there to write about it?

No one would want to have such a sad life presented to him.

Everyone would want to forget such a sad life.

As always my doubts were of no avail.

Erika is writing this book.

She will remember what I said when it is too late. When no one wants to read her book.

Would Hilde one day read the book?

"Hardly."

Hilde preferred to read stories about people who experienced something.

Had Erika's face relaxed upon hearing this answer? Besides I know my own life.

It was too close. It nearly reached the truth behind the shadows.

The questions of the daughter are becoming bothersome. Why should I think about my childhood? I learned after all from the time I was little: the only way to survive is to forget. Forget the unjust punishments. Forget the hopes that I had relinquished. Forget the contents of day dreams. Other than the one which I lived. Which I lived with you. Forget the shame of poverty. The derision stemming from it. The smell of the house. The loneliness in the damp bedroom. The desire to be able to LEARN.

Forget Hannes. Forget the cold February.

At first because of the command of the adults. Forget what you have heard. What you have seen. Forget it! But soon it was no longer necessary to shout this command into her. Soon this command of all the other people became her own. Soon she would pass on this command to others.

To whom should I give this command? To whom?

Erika is supposed to be writing a book about you and me. I would like to read this book.

And I would also like to talk about the two of us.

So why do I tell Erika about the time before you came into my life? In order to keep my expectations alive also for the time when she is visiting me?

In order not to wait out the time silently when I will be alone again?

What else should I talk to Erika about? There are no longer any long discussions. Erika does not like talking to me.

Unlike you I don't allow her to catch me off guard.

Hilde hardly ever complained about the communists.

All the complaining had not brought Erika to her senses. I don't want to hear anything about them from Erika. From a daughter who has been influenced. She would worship just any one's opinions. Would never allow herself to be convinced that she was fooled by big words.

Don't give Erika any catchwords.

Be silent.

When Erika begins with that.

Cover up her words.

With a good meal. With wine. With television.

Why didn't you forbid Erika to do that? Why not?

But she really did not actually want to talk to Erika about the relationship between Erika and Anton.

Her everyday trivialities. Should she talk about them to Erika? Erika already knew about them. Who lived alone. As she does. She could tell Erika about the latest news from the housing project. Maybe she would like such news again. That Mrs. G. and the chaplain have a relationship. Erika should write about it in her book. Why didn't Erika want to hear about such matters.

She saw the daughter wrinkling her brow. Shaking her head. Turning away from her. She would sit next to her but turn away.

As if the daughter were better than she.

And Erika?

Why didn't Erika talk more?

She couldn't possibly just work.

She had to live once in a while too.

Erika took after you in this regard.

Work was all that there had been for Anton. His work which gained recognition. Erika on the other hand. — What could Erika expect from her work?

And what does Erika get from me?

I was always there for her.

She only saw you for short periods. You played with her in the evening. As if Erika were the boy you had wanted. You made it easy for yourself. You behaved as if your wish had been granted. And Erika went along with it. Played games with him which girls actually don't play. Put together the model train with Anton. Went with him to the soccer field on weekends. Followed his orders: A boy doesn't cry. Put pants on.


I, I had to sew the pants. But these few hours couldn't balance out the many hours during which I was at home with Erika. You were surprised later on. When Erika didn't want to take dancing lessons. Then you wanted to exchange the boy for a girl. Hilde would have liked to have taken dancing lessons. But she never got any money for that. Once a boy from choir invited her to a dance. She had run into the woods howling. Had left the embarrassed lad standing alone in front of the church.

What should I have worn dancing? Wooden slippers? In order to be laughed at?

Or barefoot? Like the ugly duckling. The one who is made fun of.

And in my one and only Sunday dress? That I hated. Dark blue with a white collar.

She had to take the collar off the dress every Sunday evening in front of the mother. Had to wash, iron and sew it on again.

Dark blue. With a white collar. A sack. Which was passed on from one daughter to the next. Every Sunday morning she slipped into this sack. Went into the village. To church.

Never went dancing.

The boy had not asked her again.

It had been a long time since any boy had asked her.

Should she tell that to Erika. Erika who only wore sweaters.

Who never wanted to iron blouses.

Erika, who didn't know the secret of dancing.

Maybe she would only laugh about the unlived dances of her mother.

Would become tired. Tired of all that which was to be forgotten. Would not want to get involved with that. Not want to be bound to this self I had become. That I must remain being. Whether remembered or forgotten. The difference lies in the pain. The pains of remembering. — The emptiness after forgetting is pleasant in comparison. Pleasant — ? — This feeling of becoming COLD. Maybe death had begun with some people in this manner. —That they became COLD.

The cat had warmed up Hilde's bed. Just as Hilde had often warmed up his bed. When he came up to bed, Hilde slipped over into her bed. Sometimes when he was not too tired, he would say: "Stay a while."

Can there be words that I will never hear again?

Every bed was too large for her all alone.

She saw herself disappear in it. Not emerge from it again.

At least she had been able to stretch out her hand toward him. She had been able to hear his breathing next to her. She had been able to hope.

Then the last night had come.

The night, in which I DESERTED you.

She had turned around once more in the hospital room door. Had seen him lying there. In the large white bed. Eyes wide open. "There is no point in thinking of sleep."

The lips dried out. The body which had become so alien was visible under the thin blanket.

She had cried outside. All the nights she had spent alone. All the nights which had been spent in two beds. Those were not her nights. With difficulty Hilde now had to turn them into her nights. In order not to relinquish memories of Anton into the shadows.

The cat purred. Hilde pressed it to her. As she had pressed her child to her. When it had still been her child. When he had not yet taken it from her.

You?-You couldn't take anything from me. You belonged to me. Just like the child.

Perhaps if I snuggle up to the cat, the shadows will have no room.

But the shadows drove into her. Drove her away from the cat. Drove her-there-as they did every night. Onto the side of the GUILTY.

The cat sensed her disquiet. Jumped out of bed. LEFT her ALONE with the shadows.

Calling after the cat didn't help.

"Then scram! You beast!"

When she had finally fallen asleep, dreams tormented her. The dreams waited until the shadows made way for them.

Many people squeezed into the living room. Hilde laughed. Waited on her guests. She was NEEDED all the time. The movements of the people in the room meshed with one another. They all wore thin veils. In coordinated colors. Suddenly Anton stood in garish green pajamas in front of her. Called out in a shrill voice. That he couldn't work with so much noise. That she shouldn't squander his money for her parties. His hard-earned money. It would be better if she were there for him. Not for these strangers. These strangers, who only made his house dirty. — His house! No one took notice except her. Hilde looked at him with guilty feelings. Looked down at herself. Saw how the spots on her dress turned into holes. — Anton had always wanted a tidy wife. Her eyes were pulled away from the holes. Toward the door. Through the crack in the door crept long white flames toward her. She began to scream. Couldn't scream louder than Anton. Could do nothing to combat his irritation. Which became greater. Because she did not look at him. Rather looked past him. Had to look past him. — there — Where the floor was covered with a white flame.

When she woke up, the bed next to hers was empty. No voices were to be heard in the house.

Have all the others except me been burned to death?

She saw the cat rolled up lying at her feet. Forgot the dream. The memories of real encounters with him took the dream's place. How she had ABANDONED Anton in his illness. In order to meet Anna. Or to go shopping with Mrs. Roth. She had faced his long illness impatiently. She had interrupted her work for him impatiently. The work which she did only for him. Continually finding new dishes to cook for him. Making sure the house was cleaner than ever. The garden tended better than ever. Her guilty conscience about her absent-minded presence had been preserved in shadows and dreams. What good was it, this awareness. She had sat with Anna in the kitchen. Had tried to figure out what Anton's illness could be. A guilty conscience about Anton. Who meanwhile lay alone on the living room couch. Who waited for her. He did not talk about his illness. One was not permitted to talk about his illness. She had to nurse a healthy person.

How does one nurse a healthy person?

Maybe I did everything wrong.

Get up! Get out of bed! Quickly.   Forget this thought. Forget it!

When visitors came, he had looked at her pleadingly after a short while. She had understood. Had sent the visitors away with excuses. Had warmed his hands. Evenings. In front of the television. Had inconspicuously helped him to climb the steps. Had sensed from all his movements how much he NEEDED her. Only her.

But you didn't laugh with me. You only laughed with your daughter. You laughed occasionally, but only with your daughter.

Hilde had sprung up at this laughter. Had left the living room.

Had hated her daughter.

Neither of them was aware that she no longer sat with them.

During breakfast Hilde tries to organize her day. To give herself some order.

She stands leaning on the kitchen wall. Looks into her wine glass.

I have to think about what I absolutely must attend to today.

I must do something.

If I don't pay attention, everything gets lost in negative matters. Why tend to the garden? You would no longer go out and admire it. And why cut the grass? It no longer needs to impress the neighbors. They can no longer complain to you about me. And why clean the windows? I will no longer wait for you.

Look away. From the kitchen table. From the table which is too large for one person all alone.

Whenever Hilde persuaded herself to cook, he sat there at the table. Waiting for his meal. Sometimes he looked at her. From far away. Most of the time his head was hidden behind a newspaper.

If I could at least lose sight of the newspaper. So that you would sit there. But even the wine does not help me with that. I must not allow myself to begin drinking wine at an ever earlier hour each day as my way out.

If you were to see me in this way. How I open up a new bottle of wine now in the morning.

But you never saw me do so. Will never see me do so.

Only I had to look at such pictures from my childhood on. No one was spared in this hole in which I grew up. I had to watch father drinking hard cider there at breakfast. Had to listen to him as he vomited over and over early in the morning. My own body became alien to me there. Even before I could get to know it. I had to breathe in the reek of alcohol. All during the long cold months. And watch, as the face of the father became more bloated with each passing year. And to watch how the brothers imitated the father.

Except for Hannes. But Hannes died.

Anton had not known that. She had tried to keep it from him. Was afraid he would turn away from her. Would not distinguish between her and the others. Only when she was pregnant, had she once taken Anton into the house. Had begged before the visit that the father would refrain for once, only this once, from drinking.

Had not been able to prevent it.

Had felt how her body tightened up because of shame. How words pasted her mouth shut. How eyes became blind. Had sat next to Anton in the kitchen. At the old large table which passed the father's heavy movements onto the others. Had not heard anything except the gurgling sound when the hard cider ran down his throat.

Had looked at the mother who immediately looked away. Had not dared to look at Anton. Then she had gone with him to the train. Walked alongside him. This endless way. Had looked up to him only when he was on the train. But then it was too late. Then he no longer looked back at her. Had enough to do to find a seat. She would gladly have comforted him. She had to wait outside. She remembered the child. Wanted to call out to him: "I am giving you a child." The way she had read it in novels. Had only been able to shout out: "We are expecting a child." And was amazed only now that she had shouted we. Knew only now that she had had the courage to shout this sentence because she believed he would no longer hear her voice in the noise of the train. She could not run fast enough. Fast enough for the train.

But she must have run fast enough. Must have shouted loud enough for the train. The next day he picked her up from work. Wanted her to go away from there. To be with him.

It was then I swore to you, for your sake, never to touch a drop of alcohol. I haven't kept the promise.

But I never drank alone before. Only with you. In the evening. Our bottle of wine.

You never said anything. Except when I got too jolly. Then you reminded me quietly of the father.

Your words reach me even now. Reach the furthest corners of the room. There is no room for me. All the space has been occupied by your words. I will rinse them away. Deep down. So that they can no longer torture me.

Just today I must stop drinking. Just today. Otherwise I cannot go to the Retirees Union this evening. That much I owe you. That I continue to behave in such a way that no one can complain about me. Yes. I owe you that.

To go to you. So that this day can begin. To ask you for your forgiveness. For the weaknesses. For which you always forgave me. But you never understood them. And I could not ask that of you. You learned to be hard. To be hard with yourself. Took yourself as an example. Never asked more of others than you asked of yourself. Even I learned to set you as my model. Only I could never measure up to you, don't you see . . . And you got larger and larger next to me. In my eyes. And during the long last period it looked as if you would be able to understand me after all. That makes your death all the more difficult for me. Only at the end did it really become good. As good as I know it only from novels.

She went into the garden. Cut flowers for him. Looked for a candle. Got her bicycle out of the garage. Rode to him. No matter where she rode. Thought that she had it good with this goal. That she had it good in general. Until her feet lost contact with the pedals. The goal constantly moved further away. Her rides no longer resembled those of a year earlier. Loneliness also ate up the rides. Made them empty and strenuous. Sometimes Hilde even missed her goal.

— which goal —

Then there was no way to catch hold of herself. Then the only security was the realm of shadows. That surrounded her in the evening. Then that was too little.

Then I would prefer to plunge immediately into the chaos. Then a day which has begun in this way will not get better. It would fasten itself to me and not let me loose.

When Hilde pushed her bike into the garage, she heard the telephone ringing. She let go of her bike. Did not notice how the broken spoke hurt her knee. Ran into the house.

"Erika."

The conversation was much too short. Every conversation with her. What should she tell the daughter over hundreds of miles. She couldn't begin just anywhere. If she did not choose the beginning of her sentences carefully, one sentence pulled the next sentence along. Didn't know where the sentences were pulling her.

The daughter wanted to come by on the weekend. After all she could tell her everything on the weekend.

Erika should move in with me. She can write her book here just as well. Probably it is even better for her. If she has me around her all the time. Not just on some weekends. Such short weekends. Too short for getting to know one another again. For making a mutual silence out of the silence.

Hilde noticed the cut on her leg. The blood left a trace down to her foot. She had to sit. The cat came. Smelled the blood. Hilde pushed it way.

I have to distract myself from the blood.

The union meeting. If I want to go there, I have a lot to do: Go to the hairdressers. Buy a new dress. I know about people. No one can take issue with me about anything. People are just waiting for me to make a mistake. In order to gossip about me once again. I will not give them the opportunity.

Not today.

Never again.

For the first time in years I will be going out alone.

Going out alone? — I can't do that.

I was never able to do that.

I could say that I am sick.

No. I can't say that. I was just outside.

If I don't go today, I can never go again. And if I never go, they will criticize me. Without you it is much more difficult not to be gossiped about.

Without you everything is much more difficult.

To get a sense of security from the mirror.

Leave the house slowly. Keep thinking that I can leave any time.

Lock the door. Put the key away. Ride slowly to the inn in which she had never been. Stay calm. Nothing would remind her here of Anton. Go in. Look around carefully. For Mr. Funk.

Find him in the back of the room. Having to go up to him among all these people. Greeting him. Being introduced by him. Shaking hands. Realizing that there are more women here than men. Realizing it with an increasing CHILL. This picture whereby people become distinguishable. She ordered wine. Sat down with the women whom she knew from grocery shopping. To dull her cramped stomach with wine. Breathe slowly. Listen. Talk. Be gay. Talk about the daughter. About the distant city in which Erika lives. Listen as other sons and daughters are talked about. The proud voices when the grandchildren were talked about. Hilde did not have a grandchild. Words of consolation. She didn't need this kind of consolation. Let the center of attention go back to the grandmothers.

Hilde didn't notice how the musicians had meanwhile unpacked their instruments.

The anxiety came back with the music. The kind of anxiety which Hilde knew would stay with her.

To have to listen to dance music alone. — She had never wanted to experience that again.

Anton had also played in a dance-band.

During the time that was granted us.

He played at every ball. At every party. Until the party ended.

Your party.

Never my party.

I sat all the while at a table and listened to you. I liked to listen to you. Until there was no more for me to hear. — For me.

There was only something to see.

How you danced with another woman.

You never danced with me. Never.

Hilde had jumped up. Had tipped over her glass. Had forgotten to pay for her wine. Was seen. Was gossiped about. As she ran home.

But it was after all just a big mistake.

You up there. Me down here. You were able to see how I sent every dancer away. Were never able to see why. Assumed that I didn't want to dance. Had to assume it. By chance the other woman came up to you on the stage. I didn't see it. For once I wasn't looking up at you.

Such a simple thing. You told me about it late at night.

And Hilde now sat alone again in the hall. Had to watch as Mr. Funk smiled at his wife. Had to see how women danced with women.

Women as dance partners.

Hilde felt her hands become moist.

I don't want to dance with a woman.

You can't expect that of me.

She remained sitting alone at her table.

Didn't want to remain sitting all alone either. Didn't want to trace the design of the table with her eyes. Until they were full of tears. Didn't want to be at home in this repressed body. Wanted to dance. With Anton. At last to dance with Anton. Didn't want to have to watch the dancers. As she had done earlier. When the mother had been among the dancers. When the mother had lain on the dance floor. On the creaking wooden floor, which the owners of the house had set up in the back courtyard. Did not want to see herself. How she had stared out through the kitchen window. Had stared through all the others. Saw the father coming at the far end of the dance floor. Saw the father go up to the mother. Saw the father kick the mother. Didn't want to see how the mother ran away from the father. Ran into the kitchen. Was kicked more in the darkness. Hilde had tried not to breathe. To forget herself. But even that was not enough. I am being kicked. I. Not the mother. No. The mother. No. I. I. We are both being kicked. When the father had stopped kicking them, when they were both covered with bruises, when she crept into bed with the mother, yes crept, since she couldn't walk because of pain, the mother comforted her, comforted her by simply allowing Hilde to cuddle up to her warm soft skin, so that her skin burned less, he stumbled into the bedroom after another liter of hard cider and shouted them apart. Had ripped them apart. Had shouted words at them which Hilde had since forgotten. Which continued to hurt her. As if the sound had penetrated her body. Never left her body again. And then she knew only that she had never touched the mother's body again, and never crept under the blanket to her again.

Hannes had taken over that role.

When Hannes died, there was no blanket for me for a long time.

No blanket. Until you came along. With you there I could once again creep under a blanket. Only with you did I get WARM again.

The bruises shimmered even now through the dresses of the dancing women. Hilde heard the men shouting at their wives at home. Heard them beating their bodies. Their soft bodies. Which swallowed the loud sound of the beating. Made soft beatings out of them all.

The beatings of the father continued. On the mother's body. On her body.

The same beating hands continue. Father's hands. Mother's hands. Men's hands. — Above all the latter.

If only you were sitting next to me. If you were to dance once, only once with me. Then this anxiety would no longer exist. Only you and I would exist.

Did you LEAVE me ALONE?

Did you DESERT me?

In the intermission Hilde got up. Excused herself with a headache. She was not accustomed to so many people any more. Shook everyone's hand. Moist. Like her own hands.

Breathed relief. Breathed relief every time that she arrived home. The cat crawled around her feet. Didn't let Hilde out of sight. It was good that there was something there. That could comfort her. This necessary consolation.

Go down into the cellar

Anton is mirrored in the wine.

Drink it up. No mirrored reflections.

Think about our daughter.

Think happily about our daughter.

This joy. — It must last for days.

Erika arrived early on Friday.

As always the daughter was dressed impossibly. Swallow my anger. My anger that I have shown too often. That did not change a thing.

Erika looked tired. She drank a few cups of coffee. Didn't want to lie down. Hilde put her wine glass away unobtrusively. Fetched a cup for herself.

I don't like coffee at all.

Erika's empty gaze. It frightens me. I can never fill up this emptiness.

Nonetheless it is good that she is here. Yes, it is good that I am not so alone.

Should I tell her that I have become a member of the Retirees Union. Then she will ask questions. She can never just listen. Other people can do that. I told Mrs. Roth. She didn't make any comment. But she always thinks of something.

I already hear her questions. Since when have you been interested in politics? Oh. That has nothing to do with politics? Haven't they asked you yet whether you might not want to become a member of the Austrian Socialist Party?

No. I don't want to hear her questions. These questions which are so matter-of-fact with her. And I don't want to have to quarrel with this tense body. She can't ever keep her hands still. But she can drink coffee.

Why can't I start to talk. About how often the days are so long for me. Despite the television in the morning. And in the evening. But Erika would perhaps not understand. She is talking about how she wears herself out with her work. And about her anxiety of losing her position. If she were to live with me, she would not need to work. Then she would not need to be anxious. I would do everything for her. She could write all day long. And in the evening she would have time to watch television with me.

Should I ask her right away.

Or will the question maintain the tension — maintain it the entire weekend.

It is probably better if I ask her later when we have gotten used to one another again. Why doesn't this idea occur to her. Why doesn't she ask me. Whether she can move into her room again. Into this large room which is not lived in.

What keeps her with those strangers.

They cannot possibly replace a mother.

I would also see to it that she lives healthier. Working so late at night. That would not happen here. That's never been allowed here. If it hadn't been for me she would have read straight through the night as a child. Would have ruined her eyes. All those books.

Her room in the strange city. I could never stand that room. Books on the walls. Books everywhere. Only space for books. Here she would have a proper room, one in which we both had enough space.

"I am going to drive into the village."

Hilde got up. Looked around. Tried to find a place for the daughter's sentence.

"I want to take a look again at the village this weekend. Are you coming along?"

I know that tone.

She is going to drive.

I can come along.

I don't want to come along.

I want us to stay here. Only here can I show her how good she would have it here with me. Besides I don't want to leave the cat alone for so long.

This cat. It hasn't become accustomed to me yet. It jumped immediately into the daughter's lap. And the grave! I must visit the grave every day.

She knows the village. Knows the house. Knows all the stories about it.

But as usual the daughter didn't give in. She was prepared to go alone. If Hilde didn't want to come along. She doesn't even bother to ask.

Hilde could only complain. About the pace. About the bad food in the inns. About the beds which are much too soft in such places.

I can't actually ask her why she prefers to spend time in the village more than with me. I can't ask her anything.

# 10

Erika waited in her car for Hilde.

Hilde was annoyed.

The village inhabitants would not follow this small car with their eyes.

No one would see how well I am doing. If we had ridden in my large car, all the village would have had to see how well I am doing. How good it was for me to go away.

I was the one after all who managed to leave the village. Everyone else is still here.

No one stays willingly in the village. In the house. Except for the farmers. But no one from her house had become a farmer. No area farmers had married anyone from her house. Hilde had not even been able to dream of that. Not even when the scraps from the harvested fields and the fallen fruit had become the only source of food for the family. Brown, work-hardened hands of children. Sore backs. From harvesting potatoes. Shocking images. At home the mother's despair.

Hunger.

That was before the war.

That was when the father was a different man.

Still a proud father.

A father for whom a sense of pride was more important than hard cider.

A father who didn't want to have anything to do with politics. She had forgotten this other father.

Not his law.

Absolute law.

Only his daughter had not felt bound to the law. To the old secure law.

The father's pride was injured daily. These walks to find work which sapped his energies. The many walks. So often in vain. In vain also the shame of lingering poverty. His attempt to wash it down with large swallows.

Once poverty was connected to hope for Hilde. Fritzi, who was part of the household, was assigned to a farmer. Fritzi hoped that the farmer would marry her during the year in which the government assigned her to work on his farm. She needed someone whom she could tell of her hopes. Paltry sentences. Every Sunday. Wrapped up sentences. Every Sunday. Bacon. Eggs. Bread. Vegetables.

Fritzi came every Sunday.

Waiting for Fritzi was a nice secure waiting.

Hilde also hoped. Hoped every Sunday when she brought Fritzi's gifts into the kitchen that the mother would forget her brother and above all Monika. That she would caress her hair in front of all the others.

The unfulfilled hopes of that year. —What to do with them.

Fritzi married my brother Max.

I threw my hope away.

Should I tell that to Erika? Better not. Better to look into the river or to observe the chain of hills. The river and the hills, I am used to them.

Around the next curve the village lay before them.

Hilde saw the old pear tree on which Hannes

— my Hannes —

had hung.

February-tree.

Unchanged ever since. Leafless branches. Fruitless branches. The earth covered with snow. With slushy snow. Many imprints of boots. Even today. On this hot summer day. Erika wanted to know more about Hannes' death.

More?

The foolishness of the daughter.

"I can't tell you more. I couldn't ask him: Why did you go to the tree."

Somehow everything is very blurred. At first there was so much noise. After that no one was permitted to talk about Hannes, nor about his death.

Someone in uniform had waited for her at the school. Had lead her away from the other children. Had asked her about Hannes. While the other children left the schoolyard. Had left her standing alone in the schoolyard. Had shouted to her from the street: "Your brother is dead! Be careful, that the same doesn't happen to you."

The next day the father was already at home at noon. Silently he had hung his blue work shirt on the hook on the back of the kitchen door. Silently he had put on his uniform. The uniform which Pesendorfer had thrown into the kitchen. He had eaten silently. Had left the house as an overseer of a group of prisoners of war. He said one thing. As soon as he reached the hall. "Nazi pigs."

Cursed them a second time through his badly broken teeth.

The mother's frightened look in the hallway.

Hilde's confused look.

Silence.

Actually we never talked about Hannes.

She had run across the meadow after the threatening words in the schoolyard. In her haste she had lost a wooden shoe in the snow. Forgot her anger about it. Knew only that she must get home. Get home to Hannes. That stopped her feet short before she knew why.

The house tenants were standing in the yard. The black uniforms stood in front of them. Pesendorfer blocked the house door. She had to go past him. In order to get into the house. Into her room. To Hannes. Would have to ask him to let her in. Would perhaps have to ask him against all odds, him of all people. Would perhaps have rubbed against his uniform. If he would have given her too little room. Like the other tenants her parents stood in front of the black uniforms. No.

She never wanted to go back home again.

Not to this group of people. Which Hannes could not join.

Then she had run into the forest over there. Had lain down in the snow. Waited. For death in the snow. Better to freeze to death. Than to be a part of that group again. The slow death of the snow. There was so much time. Time during which the mother could look for her. During which the mother looks for her. The mother finds her.

Hilde had wanted to be found dead. Until the uniforms had left the house. She went back to the house tired. The mother sat at the kitchen table. Had her head propped in her hands. Did not look up. The father shouted at her. Why did she come so late? Added: "Hannes is dead."

Shadows came into the kitchen.

Shadows waited in the room for her. To comprehend beyond the shadows. To have to comprehend it forever. The man dressed in black hadn't lied to me. Hannes is really dead. He would never be with me under one blanket, would never STUDY with me again.

She had enough to do to figure out with whom she should STUDY now.

Erika had asked few questions. Had let the direction be determined for her.

Hilde went down the path from the village to the house.

That this house was still inhabited. No cellar. Moist thick walls. Water in the hall. From the fall until the summer the light had to be on even during the day. Nonetheless the room never actually became bright enough. There was one outdoor toilet in the yard for all the house tenants. The long waiting in front of it every morning.

Hilde and Erika had sat a few minutes on the old wooden bench. On the side open to the yard stood the same small gardens. For every apartment one garden. Hilde became restless on the house bench. She got up. Walked away.

When they no longer saw the house, she breathed easily. Now she could tell Erika her story about the garden. Mrs. Emmerich had planted strawberries there. And bragged about it. And told everyone how well the strawberries grew. They were red and ripe. Red spots on the green. "Red was also once my color."

Hilde smirked. Looked quickly at the daughter. Was surprised that the daughter had nothing to say.

The flaming red. A prettier color the children of the house had never seen. They never quarreled anymore. They wanted strawberries.

One day a week Mrs. Emmerich did her grocery shopping. Fritzi watched her walk away. Then the children fulfilled their desire. No more red on the green.

Hilde was glad that Erika laughed with her about the indignant face of Mrs. Emmerich. About the inquisition of the father. About the children's lips which were pressed together.

So they were all involved.

The father's response. Every child got a spanking with the fly swatter. Mrs. Emmerich watched.

The children saw Mrs. Emmerich's satisfied face.

Hilde was even able to laugh about the spanking.

She didn't tell the daughter that. She didn't want to quarrel with her. Erika was against beatings. Maintained that she could remember every beating. Every single helplessness. Which was associated with the beating. Erika later called the beatings humiliation.

How can she know what humiliation is.

She exaggerates. As usual.

They went to the old pond, which had been used for putting

out fires. The children had bathed there although they were forbidden to do so. Nowadays it was no longer used. Marsh marigolds on the shore. Thick mud in the water. Green and brown. Frogs. Swarms of mosquitoes. Behind that the old picture. Much stronger than the new one. Heavy baskets of clothes on the shore. Hands rubbed red in the summer. Lifeless hands rubbed red in the cold period. The mother bent over the border of stones which were no longer visible. Hilde beside her.

Bent down.

Despicable work.

Dreams were of no use. Dreams became meaningless.

Wash days were endless.

And other days.

Sometimes Hannes had helped them carry the wash. Took one basket from them. Brought it to the pond. Had fetched the next one. No other brother had ever helped with the housework. The mother had never dared to make demands on her sons.

She made demands on her daughters.

At first on all three.

Until Renate moved in with her grandparents. Until Monika broke down. Wash days became longer then. And the days on which Hilde had to clean the outdoor toilet and the house hallway. This old treaded wood. The many rills in the wood.

To kneel on the floor. With the dirt in the furrows she felt the need to vomit.

"Tell me something about Monika."

"There isn't much to say about her. She was two years older than I. And was different. Had such pale skin. And long light-colored hair. No one knew where she had gotten her looks from. She was quiet. At some time or other she remained in bed. Didn't get up again. Never again. And she was proud of her hair. She often laughed at me. I would never have such pretty hair as she had. Then she laughed as I had never heard her laugh before."

Hilde viewed Monika as a figure from her dreams. She didn't talk about dreams. She was sure that Monika and Renate had never been beaten by the father. That she had hated her sisters for that reason. She had hated her sisters above all because they stood between her and the mother.

Maybe my sisters were the first to LET me DOWN. To ABANDON me.

Renate went to her grandparents when she was ten years old. I was only six. I never saw her again. And Monika went to bed. Never got up again. Never spoke a word with me. Not a word. Never ate. Never drank.

Simply fell asleep.

Monika didn't NEED me.

Just as my daughter doesn't NEED me. Sits next to me and stares in the dirty pond. In which she can see nothing. She could sit here alone just as well. When she knows almost no questions to ask me.

And doesn't talk to me. I won't talk to her either. I don't NEED her.

I only NEEDED you. And you NEEDED me. But I don't want to think about that today. Today everything centers on me. But how can everything center on me? If I am not asked anything.

What did my daughter expect?

This woman. For whom it is enough to cross the meadow. To lean on fruit trees. She, who has no memories attached to these fruit trees. What was there here for her to see. That her eyes never became empty.

Hilde wanted to go to the tavern. Silently they walked next to one another down the promenade of cider apple trees. Hilde's way to school. Even today not paved. She can feel the cobblestones on the soles of her feet. Can imagine bending down quickly for apples. For these little, bitter apples. The teacher had waited for the children everyday at the entrance to the schoolyard. When she was among those children whom he greeted by stroking their hair, then her feet didn't hurt. These sore feet.

Hilde sensed that Erika was no longer walking beside her. She turned around. Saw Erika standing next to the barn.

My daughter is ruining everything for me today. Even my memories of the ONLY teacher who never beat us. Who played with us. Who laughed sometimes. With us. For two years.

One day they came to school and there was no teacher waiting for the children. A stranger sat in the classroom. One whom they couldn't ask. Whose mouth and hand touched the children in a hard angular way.

I often stood next to the barn where she is standing now. From that position I looked in that direction over — there —. Where I did not want to look. Where I was not permitted to look.

And once I was in the barn.

Once.

Since then, never again.

That barn.

Keep walking.

I must keep walking.

She'll follow me.

She won't go into the barn without me.

She won't look over-there-without me.

Erika came up to Hilde, slowly. The memory had vanished from Hilde's face. When she saw the daughter coming up to her with her head bowed. Instead of memory a short triumphant smile at the thought that the daughter had waited in vain. And that the daughter NEEDED her! Even when she didn't want to admit that.

For without me this — there — is a — there — like any other.

It's the same way with me, too.

Why should it matter to me.

Everyone was able to look from the barn over -- there --. And what does my daughter's interest mean to me. Her questioning glances. One can't overlook it.

I can leave thoughts about this place — there — , about such places — there — to her. This woman, in whom I cannot find myself. Who only consists of thoughts.

# 11

Erika lay down on the bed in the room. Looked at the ceiling. Hilde was hungry. "Let's go eat something."

Sometimes I could just hit her. When she's so absent-minded. Doesn't give in. Doesn't even give in to a request of the mother.

Eat alone in the restaurant? Expose myself to all the stares? I might as well drive away alone now.

Erika only thinks about herself.

Finally she gets up.

She is a good child after all.

But she is so strange. So strange in every way. And stubborn.

I am the one who must forget. Who has to forget continuously. That she is a communist. It doesn't bother her.

A communist of all things.

When Hilde thought about it, she hated the daughter.

There had been communists in the village also.

Many.

Russians.

I got to know one, who was probably called Ivan. After all they're all called Ivan. That one came into the house. Searched through the house. Took Pesendorfer with him. Took father along with him. Without saying a word.

Only motioned with his fingers. Two other Russians arrested them. They went away with them. Father came home again in three days. He never spoke about it. I didn't ask anything. Just as no one else did either.

Only the daughter thinks she must find out everything. And the daughter doesn't understand how happy I am that I learned in time not to ask questions.

The anxiety was there before that. Was there long before that. Was there before she knew any Russians. Anxiety ran ahead of the Russians with the sentence: "Lord mercy, when the Russians come, then you'd better watch out!"

Didn't ask, what will happen. Better not to ask.

Anxiety crept through the house in February.

No one could drive it away. It lay lurking everywhere.

Ivan and his two companions had entered the house.

She had been alone with the parents. They had been sitting speechless around the large kitchen table. Each one on a different side of the table. Had remained sitting there. Until there was a knock on the door. The mother had jerked with her shoulders. Had gotten up. Had opened the door. Ivan had filled up the doorway. The father had not looked at anyone. Hilde wanted to get up. One look from the mother. Had had to remain sitting silently at the table. Wanted to go under the table. There she would not have to recognize the bundle. Nor the open van. Into which they had thrown the bundle. Couldn't go under the table. The fly swatter awaited her under the table. She had to try at least to wipe the pictures away. Wiped them away with the threat which in the meantime had been uttered in its fullness:

"Lord mercy, when the Russians come. Then all the women will be raped."

Had heard Mrs. Wagner scream. Mrs. Pesendorfer. Mrs. Emmerich. Began screaming along with them. It was better to scream immediately so that the Ivans would know the score. So that the Ivans knew that she would defend herself.

Then the mother had turned away from Ivan toward her. The mother had returned to the table.

It took so long before the mother came back to me. Unbearably long.

Even now the mother took much too much time for the few steps to the table. The mother never got there.

The mother did not understand.

The mother gave me a slap. The fat, old mother. Whom no one would rape.

She betrayed me to the Ivans.

Now the Ivans knew that they could do to Hilde whatever the Ivans wanted. Hilde knew what the Ivans wanted.

Knew it ever since she had heard the threatening sentences. The mother knew these sentences.

The mother had threatened with these sentences.

Then Hilde got up. Ran past the Ivans and headed upstairs. Ran past Mrs. Wagner. Mrs. Wagner who was screaming. Past Mrs. Pesendorfer. Mrs. Pesendorfer, who was screaming. Screaming.

Had let the door close behind her. Had let herself fall on the bed. Had waited for the hand. The strong hand. Which would place itself on her shoulder. Which would turn her around. Which would make everything she had heard true. Because all threats had come true in the last years. Only the threats had come true. The hand came. Was strong. Had laid itself on her shoulder. Had turned her around.

Ivan had looked at her. Had said: "Stupid girl. You don't have to cry."

Then Ivan was gone. There was talking again in the house. And yet it remained quiet.

Hilde had overheard later in a restaurant like this one about why the father had returned home immediately. The prisoners of war, for whom he was responsible, had all testified for him. It was hard to understand this from the acid remarks of the men. They talked of cowardliness and betrayal.

Pesendorfer did not return to the house. Mrs. Pesendorfer moved away. And no one asked where she went. The house, which usually was porous, even for unspoken words, was also silent.

*Elisabeth Reichart*

# 12

Hilde no longer knew anyone in this restaurant. The guests stared for a short time when the two women came in.

All the heads had turned toward them at the same time. The right hands took hold of the glasses. Took the glasses to the mouth. Put them back on the table firmly. All the heads turned away from them again.

As if they had practiced this choral response.

When Hilde and Erika looked up they looked into men's eyes.

They ate hastily. Hilde asked the waiter if he could have a bottle of wine sent to their room.

"This is not a hotel." He disappeared grinning. Came back with a bottle. Swung the bottle back and forth. Now everyone grinned.

I will have to carry this bottle past their grins.

I alone.

Erika waited outside.

Is she ashamed of me as I was ashamed of the father? But that was something totally different after all. He drank hard cider for breakfast. Had on principle only drunk hard cider. The sour smell had clung to the kitchen. And when there was no money, he sent me begging to the farmers. Because it was not as easy for them to say no to me, the girl, as it was to say no to him.

The farmers had laughed when they saw Hilde coming. Had sometimes sent her away without hard cider. Had sometimes poured some of it into her jug. Mockingly. There were many reasons for such shame. Shame for her father. Shame for the farmers. And at the same time also shame for herself. Because she went nonetheless. Because she asked — with a voice made small — . Let herself be laughed at and touched momentarily rather than be beaten.

Her father waited on the house bench. When she came back from the peasants without hard cider, he pulled her by the hair into the kitchen. Let the fly swatter smack against her. This smacking. Before the leather hit her skin.

This smacking. Even later on. When she was no longer beaten. "Traitor," he upbraided her. Screamed at her. He knew precisely, he said, that she had only waited behind the house. Instead of obeying him. "But as long as you sit at my table I'll beat obedience into you." Even so she had hidden behind the house only the first time. Under the rotten table. Had tried beforehand to go across the big meadow to the farmyard. Had not been able to go. Then she had never been able to hide again. The father had stood suddenly in front of her. Was so angry that he forgot, what he emphasized with all the beatings of the fly swatter: that he never beat his kids with his hands. Never beat with such nice hands. Because his kids were not worthy of such nice hands. Were not worthy of these slender long fingers. Which he often looked at. Which even amazed him. Which had to be something special. With his bloated fat body.

When he had had to put on the army uniform instead of his workman's coat, he had stretched out his hands in front of him. Had looked at them a long time. Had consoled himself or his hands. "Have no fear. You will not have much to do."

Whether it was really because of his hands that the prisoners of war were able to vouch for him? Because of these hands. Without a stain.

It is good that I went away from the village. Away from all the knowing stares. All the same whether she knew whose eyes they were or not. The daughter will never see these men again. She does not know these knowing stares. But she turns away from me anyway because of such a trivial matter.

Prefers to wait outside for me.

She, who never had any reason to be ashamed of her parents.

Only I have had to be ashamed of everyone.

Even of my daughter. But she doesn't understand that.

The shame that has arisen from the dead. That arose with
the daughter's first boyfriend. Before that even the
disappointment. That she didn't tell her anything about
him. She had to learn of the disgrace from others. How
little a child knew its mother. A mother who perceives
every expression on a daughter's face. Every new expression. A mother who hears the gossip. Before it can spread.
"Erika is going out with one of the men from the army
barracks. Your Erika can't find a better man than one from
that place."

At least in this case, you sided with me.

At least this once you listened to me.

Anton had had the convincing discussion with his daughter.

That she must STUDY. That he would take her out of
school, if she didn't STUDY well. That she didn't have
time for a boyfriend. If it was absolutely necessary, then
she could become friends with a fellow pupil. He would
understand that. She could STUDY with a fellow pupil. Or
she could go to the theater. A man from the army barracks
would surely not go to the theater with her. He surely only
wanted one thing from her. They are like that. She can't
change that. She could never like someone so much that
she would be able to change someone from there.

And their daughter?

Their daughter had challenged her parents. Had believed she had to be ashamed of them. Had not seen how much her parents were ashamed on her account.

Why did I go away from the village and the house. Surely not so that the daughter could go back into such a house. Into an army barracks.

The army barracks no longer existed. Torn down. Replaced. With brick houses.

And how had their daughter replaced the army barracks? Gone from the barracks to writing books. As if that could provide women the possibility to get along in life. She acts as if there were no unwritten laws for us women. Takes this path. Which is only an iridescent ball. Which she herself blew into shape. Just like earlier. When she was a child. She will suffocate in her paper mountains. Then it is too late. For the right path. For the path of all women.

Hilde observed Erika. How she unpacked her typewriter. Put it on the little table in front of the window. Left the mother alone in the room.

*February Shadows*

# 13

Why isn't she writing?

Why does she just sit there with her back bent over?

No sound, only this back.

The bed is left to me. Or this chair which is standing alone in the room.

Hilde washes out her toothbrush glass. Pours herself some wine. Goes to the window. She turns around in front of the daughter's back. Prefers to go back into the unknown room. Rather than stand next to the estranged daughter.

This stranger. Who has spent the day with me. Walked next to me. Ate. Drank. Why is the day different for her than for me.

That she can sit down at the typewriter.

Instead of with me.

Erika was writing now.

Could I get used to the clattering sound? Surely. If Erika were to live with me, she could write in her own room. Not so close to me.

It must be nice to be able to take one's work along everywhere. Then one is not so lonely on evenings like this one. At home we could sit down comfortably in front of the television. Here, however, there is nothing for me to do. But are there not tough hours at home too?

To work again. To work again somewhere as a saleslady. No. Erika had suggested it. Only the daughter could have such an idea. The clever daughter. Who OVERLOOKS her own mother because of all her cleverness. Can only see herself. She takes on any work. But she has her writing. She doesn't have to say: "I am an office clerk." She can say: "I am a writer." But no one would address me as they used to with Anton's academic title of doctor. I would only be a saleslady.

And besides no one would want me anyway. I am too old. Erika even says that it is getting more and more difficult to find work. No one is waiting for me. Saleslady. I never liked this occupation. I only trained to become a saleslady because I was not permitted to LEARN, what I wanted to LEARN.

I wanted to become a nurse. After the work in the infirmary. If I had STUDIED that kind of work, everything would be different. She had been good at helping. Everyone had confirmed how hard-working she was. How she sacrificed herself for the wounded. Lived only for other people. During the last few weeks. She was not frightened by the shooting. By the limbs which were shot off. Had found the right words for everyone.

Had found Anna.

Anna who NEEDED her. Who wanted to learn the Austrian dialect from her. Who did not permit any questions. No tears.

Who had disappeared one day.

As all of them had.

Whom she met years later by chance. When they no longer had to talk about how they had become acquainted.

Those people who had spoken about her courage during the last weeks, those people were gone when Hilde NEEDED them.

I fought a long time for this line of work.

No one helped me.

Her mother had only stared at her. Had shaken her head. About Hilde's dumb ideas. In addition had made her wash the dishes everyday from then on. Hilde ought to notice, that there was enough work to be done at home. These daily mountains of dirty dishes. That brown, greasy water. Don't look down into it. Don't reach down into it. Carry the heavy pot of water into the kitchen from the hall. And carry the dirty dish-water out. The father had one of his temper tantrums. "I will drive these crazy ideas out of you."

Then she had pulled her head in and had gone away. The fear of the fly swatter opposed the fear of NOT being allowed to LEARN. The experience of the fly swatter opposed the anticipation of what life would be like when there was only the house.

The vague anxiety.

All that remained was for the father to take her to the grocer in the village. He was looking for an apprentice. One who would also keep his house clean.

The father was proud of his idea. And of himself. Because the daughter would be able to LEARN something. There she would learn something. Without getting crazy ideas. All the work would prevent that. "Once and for all! I hope so. If not. If you know what I mean!" The father's triumph. Hilde's futile battle. Hilde's futile attempt.

The daughter doesn't know about that.

At first she went to the grocer's crying. Soon she recognized in herself the silent tears of her mother.

I have spent my whole life bending over dirt.

Over this hateful dirt.

Over this dirt which does not end.

Not like the daughter over white paper.

Why don't the reams of white paper become fewer in number?

If only I had work involving white paper, I wouldn't be so discontented. Be like her.

But I only learned to clean house.

Had had to clean all the time.

There was no time left to stare at white paper.

There was hardly time to curse cleaning.

Although it was a good thing that I learned how.

That I wanted cleanliness. Like you.

This noisy clattering. It does not stop on my account. It constantly stops short. Starts up again for a short while. Such a short while that I am not sure whether I really heard it. If she can't write faster, than she should let it be.

Why was the daughter permitted to LEARN everything? Whatever she wanted. Certainly not so that she could spend her life at this typewriter.

When acquaintances ask me what Erika is writing about. What should I tell them? Surely someone will ask me again soon. People always ask at that moment, when I don't want to be asked.

What should I say?

She has not been proud of the daughter for some time now. Ever since she saw the many half empty pages.

Those wastebaskets which were overflowing. Which had been stuffed full by restless hands. Ever since she observed that tense face, from which the tension never leaves. Ever since she once smoothed out the paper which had been thrown away. Had read the lines. Could not find herself in the daughter's words. As little as she could find herself in the daughter.

This woman who is dealt with in broken off sentences. I am not this woman. She is a phantom of the daughter's imagination. I never had a black cat. She never had a black cat either. Nothing but lies. And this house, which is sometimes mentioned. This house never existed. As little as the drunkard father. Or my search for the mother. And I never wanted to become a nurse. A nurse of all things. I, who can't stand the sight of blood. How long has it been since I couldn't stand the sight of blood? These everlasting questions. Erika does nothing but ask questions.

I waited for you. As long as I can remember.

They don't exist. These cats. This village. This father. This mother. This house.

Only you were reality. Only you.

It is totally ridiculous that she is writing about me. How can she write about the mother whom she doesn't know? She can't know me. Because I haven't known her for the longest time.

It is my life. Not her life. My life is no matter of concern for her. Of no concern. Why is she meddling in my life.

I was never permitted to meddle in her life. She set her mind against that. From the beginning. I, too, must learn to offer resistance. Otherwise she will take over my life. As the others did.

When she is sleeping, I will read everything.

It is important that I read everything.

Yes. Everything.

I must not let her take my life away from me.

I have so little life.

Hilde became tired. Wanted the clattering sound to finally stop. Wanted to talk to Erika. Didn't know about what.

If you were still alive, Erika wouldn't write about me.

Why doesn't she write about you. About the beloved father? And how can she write about me without writing about you?

How silly she is. If she believes she can write about my life without writing about yours.

My life. Life existed only with you. Or should she write about that? She has no right to. She has no right to think what I think. No, she doesn't.

The mysterious evening with the Pesendorfers crossed Hilde's mind again. That evening. Which they all wanted.

It must have been a February-evening shortly after the air-raids on the village. Yes. The air-raids also occurred in this month of death. Hilde had just left the path lined with the apple cider trees. When a low flying plane closed in. As if hypnotized she had stared at the plane. And incredulously.

Until then the war had sent its consequences. Prisoners of war. Foreign workers. The concentration camp. Dead people. But that had nothing to do with me.

Just as this low flying plane could have nothing to do with me.

Then a bomb hit the ground in front of her. And then another. Behind her still another. The earth disintegrated. Covered her up. Clods. Fragments. Clumps.

So that was war. This late anxiety about suffocation. That too was war. When she was able to see again, her brother Stephen lay a few meters away from her. She recognized him because of the worn out wooden shoes with the black swastika. He had greased them up. Laughingly. On one of those long Sunday afternoons. When some of the Hitler Youth had wanted to take him to their group. "Look here!" he had called to them. "Just look here. Even you are not as loyal as I am."

Stephen!

Only then did she drop her book bag.

Screamed.

Believed her screaming was louder than any scream. This screaming. Which only reached the snow. The snow melted under her. Made her clothes wet. The COLD ran into her. As once before. This time the mother found her.

Death had remained in the house in February.

Mrs. Pesendorfer had knocked on the kitchen door one evening and had asked, with an auspicious voice, whether they didn't want to take part. In the seance.

The mystery — of — that — word.

An aunt of hers had come just for that purpose.

The mother's gaze. It could have been questioning.

The father's familiar glance at his hands.

His nodding head answered the mother.

They had gone into Mrs. Pesendorfer's apartment.

Quietly.

Darkened windows. Like every evening. Only a candle on a chest lit up the room. Flickering light, when they opened the door.

The mystery — of — that — light.

The woman from the city wore a dark head scarf. Unwillingly she shook her head about the disturbance. Mrs. Pesendorfer showed them their seats. Laid a finger on her mouth. No word was permitted to be spoken. When Hilde's right hand touched the father's tender hand, she shuddered.

Our hands never touched one another so softly.

Her left hand hung on to that of her brother Max. Max had come along hesitatingly. He didn't like secrets. All of the tenants of the house had already closed their eyes. Thus the eyes of the stranger met her eyes of all people. Hilde shut her eyes too. Trusted herself to the voice who was asking: Who would be the first in the house to die.

She felt the tremor of the father's hand. Recognized the edgy outright laughter of Pesendorfer. This horrible laughter from one of the past February-nights. The table didn't move. The woman became angry. Demanded more seriousness. Asked again. Mrs. Wagner coughed then. Mrs. Emmerich joined her. The table did not let itself be disturbed any longer. It moved. Slowly. To Max. Jerked back. Jerked back and forth. Stopped in front of Mrs. Kals. In front of the silent Mrs. Kals. Whose husband was missing. Whose baby was always sick. She began to cry. Hilde wanted to get up. To comfort her. Then her eyes got entangled again with those of that woman. Paralyzed she stayed seated. Only dared to cast a short glance around the table. Wanted to know for a second if one of the adults was more courageous. No one moved. She forgot her question. Closed her eyes. Laid her hands back on the table.

Mrs. Kals cried silently. The closed circle began to move the table again. It wandered now from one person to another. Stopped in front of the stranger. The woman got up. Knocked over her chair in doing so. Scolded. There was someone in the circle who didn't trust her. Under such circumstances she could not control the table. Everyone must trust her. Not a single person was permitted to doubt her. Hilde felt guilty immediately. Sensed how the GUILT spread out in her. When she looked at the skull on Pesendorfer. The skull on his arm. It was illuminated by a flame. As if it would claim all the light for itself.

"Auntie! Everyone here trusts the Führer! There is no trust left over for you!"

Pesendorfer laid his hands on the table again.

All the hands joined his hands.

The woman picked up her chair. Sat down again. Looked at Pesendorfer apologetically. She said she would ask another question. Pesendorfer suggested she should ask the table: "Whether we are going to win the war?"

Max left the table now. Stood in front of Pesendorfer. "You skeptic. Now there are skeptics even in the Black Shirts."

Hilde looked at the father. The father didn't react. Looked at the mother. The mother had closed her eyes. But Pesendorfer stayed calm. He said he had expected such an answer from a loyal German. He was satisfied. Nodded to Max encouragingly. Looked from one to the other. Hilde thought he would only look at her.

"No one has any backbone!"

Laid his hands on the table again.

The strange woman asked who would survive the next fifty years. The table moved to Hilde right away. Stopped in front of her. The faces which had at first turned toward Hilde in a friendly manner became angry. None of them were supposed to live another fifty years?

Pesendorfer sprang up. Sprang into the insecure laughter of the others. Ordered the woman to leave the house. Otherwise he would inform on her.

He had only taken part in order to know for sure. More and more frequently they had gotten news of such pranks. The whole show was nothing but a demoralization of the civilian population.

Who were to be incapacitated before the final phase of battle. All he had to do was to look at Mrs. Kals. No wonder if she were not able to work for the winter charity drive tomorrow. When this woman did not have anything more cheery to offer than imminent death.

The woman packed her bag. Stood with an angry, unmysterious face in front of Mrs. Pesendorfer. She looked at the floor. The woman slammed the door behind her. It had been a long time since anyone had slammed a door in this house. Pesendorfer took leave of the tenants of the house with "Heil Hitler!" All the hands which had just touched one another stretched out into the cold February-air. One at a time. One at a time the tenants of the house went into their dark rooms.

Fifty years were promised.

A period of fifty years.

Maybe even more than fifty years.

This time will not be over for a long while. Fifty fateful years were guaranteed. The daughter is powerless against them.

And if the table lied?

My head starts aching from the hammering.

I could tell her about that evening. She would stop her writing right away. No. I will never tell her about it. She would only ask more about it.

"Now stop, will you!"

"Is it disturbing you?"

"Of course it disturbs me."

Erika put the typewriter away. Put the table in front of Hilde's armchair. Fetched the armchair from the window. Sat across from Hilde. Poured the rest of the wine into the other toothbrush glass.

"Why aren't you writing about your father?"

Erika looked at her astonished.

I must ask further. All the while she knows precisely what I want to know. How can anyone be as stubborn as she is? "Why are you writing about me?"

Lowers her head. Doesn't look at the daughter. When she speaks these words:

"Because I neglected you for too long."

I must keep control of myself. She must not notice anything. Why did she have to say this sentence. I didn't want to hear this sentence. I do not want to talk about it. We can talk about everything. But not about that. I must forget this sentence. Quickly.

I want to be able to continue complaining. About my life which was NEGLECTED.

That began long before she was there.

I do not want to hear that anymore. To know that someone wants to change that.

Now that you no longer exist.

Nothing can help.

Nothing is of any use.

NEGLECTED.

A mother NEGLECTED.

A daughter NEGLECTED a mother.

Always having been NEGLECTED. Even on that February-night, when everyone was seen, who did not want to be seen, I was NEGLECTED. A NEGLECTED life.

Hilde begins to laugh. Laughs into the anxious face of the daughter. Laughs the caressing hands away. Laughs the explanatory words into the night.

Goes to the window. Laughs herself into the gloom. The trusted gloom.

Her hands on my back. Her head on my shoulder.

All that just to win my favor.

The voice of a drunkard in the street. Shuffling steps. When the drunkard joins in Hilde's laughter, Hilde stops. Shuts the window.

No mutual concerns.

I want to stay ALONE.

Goes to her bag. Fetches her nightgown. Puts it on. Lies down in bed.

Today the shadows will not come. Today I am my own shadow.

# 14

Erika woke Hilde up. She had been striking out around her. Had screamed. Hilde saw the daughter's face above her. Saw the wrinkles in her face. Every single wrinkle. Wrinkles in her brow. Deep wrinkles around her eyes. Wrinkles from her nose to her mouth.

She looks old.

Hilde shut her eyes again. Felt her aching head. Wanted to stay in bed.

"Go for a walk alone."

Erika brought her coffee. Fetched her a pill from her handbag.

Why did she have pills. Who knows what she is giving me. Hilde wanted to see the package. Headache pills. She took two of them.

Erika asked Hilde to go with her. She let her ask a few more times. Watched the daughter.

Before she stops asking, I must give in.

Hilde got up. Complaining about the bad wine. Better get
up. Otherwise the day will become too long. Now that her
headache was subsiding. Erika had agreed to drive to the
river.

Hilde looked for the sand bank. It had hardly changed.
Only the river close up looked different than it had
previously. Hilde didn't want to go into the murky water.
Spread out her blanket among the willow trees. Watched
the daughter through half closed eyes. How she tried to
swim against the current. Saw that Erika could tread water.
But that was not enough for the daughter. She swam with
a powerful movement against the current. As if it were
important for her to be stronger than the river current.

Her body seemed exhilarated when she came out of the
water. Her face alert. The red spots took away some of the
sternness of her face. She lay down beside Hilde. In the
sand.

"Your hair will get knotted."

"That doesn't make any difference."

Erika let the sand run between her fingers. Hilde put her
hands into the sand too. Carefully. Shook the sand immediately off her skin again. It would just dry it out.

If I were lying here with Anna, we would chat about the
latest news. The sun wouldn't burn so. The sand wouldn't
disturb me. But with her that's impossible.

Next to her the sun burns. I feel every grain of sand on the blanket. I still haven't asked her yet.

It's never the right moment for my question. If we had stayed at home, I would surely have been able to ask her by now.

As on many hot summer days, the sky here grew dark very quickly. In a few minutes it would begin to rain. Even while they were gathering their belongings the river overflowed its banks. Flooded the sand bank.

Once Hilde had lost a towel in this way. She had gotten into the tug of the water. Had looked desperately for the towel. Had found it finally down stream hanging from a willow. Had called her brother Max: "Help me! Please!" Max had laughed at her. She should fetch it herself if she could. She had seen herself standing alone. Alone in the tugging water. Could hardly hold herself upright. Although the water reached only up to her knees. The rising water. She wanted to lie in the water. Only wanted to lie there. Then she imagined she saw Hannes. Hannes who would surely have helped her. Hannes whom she had had to help. She had gotten out of the water. Had laid down between the willow trees. Had cried into the laughter of Max and the other children. Until they found it too stupid. They went home.

Once again I was EXCLUDED.

In addition, the fear of the fly swatter. The mother's despairing look.

Tried to fight her anxiety with dreams. Some day someone would stay with her. He would fetch every towel for her out of the water. Would hand it over to her and bow. Would take her home holding her hand. As in the church song. So take my hands / lead me / till my life's end and / everlastingly.

This person would be a big, strong man. He would give Max a slap in the face. Because he hadn't helped his sister. Her brothers and sisters would have to watch how the big, strong man presented her with a pair of shoes. As soon as the shoes got old, not very old, he would come again. With pretty, new shoes. The father would be sitting soberly on the house bench. He would be proud of his daughter. All at once she would give this person a sign. For his next visit he would also have a pair of shoes for the mother. He would promise meat for the father. In exchange for the fly swatter.

From this day onward the mother would never NEGLECT her.

During the time before you came, there was still this hope for redemption.

Hilde said that they must leave. She didn't want to get wet hair. With a towel over her head she ran past the daughter, who was laughing, to the car.

"Rainwater makes one pretty!"

Hilde shook her head. No. No rain water will make you pretty. It can't rain that much.

They drove past pear trees. Drove past the turn off to the house. Drove through the old village gate. Into the village.

These thick walls. They made the streets narrow. Stand in a lonely fashion. Without a background. The few houses in the village center. They were the center of the world for me. Outside. In the house. The chestnut trees on the village square. The benches. The benches with the old women.

Wherever I go, everywhere there are these wrinkled-up, old women waiting for me.

The village square was not always so empty.

Here the village children played. Sometimes the children from the house stood at the edge. Had watched them playing.

On Sundays the men and women formed separate groups. Except for the men and women from the house. After mass they went back immediately to the house.

The people in February.

The people of the night.

# 15

They were the only guests this early in the afternoon. They could have something cold to eat. Warm meals were to be had only at noontime and in the evening. The waiter pointed to the smeared sign on the door. Hilde sat down.

Erika wanted to go to her room.

"Sit down with me."

It smelled of cold smoke and stale beer. All the windows were closed. Hilde opened the window next to her table. The waiter came. Complained. Why had he built in an air conditioner if everyone could simply open a window.

He unwillingly put a quarter liter of wine in front of Hilde. He put some coffee in front of Erika. After he had brought a cheese sandwich for Hilde, he asked whether they wanted anything else?

Erika's angry voice.

"Yes. The check."

Then they didn't say anything more.

Then there was a whispering.

Whispering from the kitchen.

Sentence fragments.

Fragments.

. . . She is the one. . .

. . . Yes, I already heard about her, yes, yes . . .

. . .One of those from the house . . .

I know which one you mean . . .

. . . what! The daughter of Schalk . . .

Oh no. . .

One of those who . . .

. . .who actually. . .

. . .that she dares to come here. . .

. . .how brazen . . .

. . . What a nerve. . .

We should. . .

"Let's go."

Hilde bit her lower lip.

Didn't look at the daughter.

They went into their room. Each sat on her own bed. Hilde sat stiffly.

Her hands crammed together.

"Get me some wine."

A sentence without emphasis.

When Erika came back with a bottle of wine, Hilde was still sitting on the bed in the same stiff way as before. Erika poured a toothbrush glass full. Handed her the glass. Began to stroke Hilde's head. Hilde's hands had a difficult time disentangling themselves. It was so strenuous. To hold this glass of wine. She needed two hands to do so.

No movement of her lips was perceivable. While she drank her wine.

"And now go.

Go away at last.

What do you want of me?

Do you want to watch me perhaps?

That happened all on your account.

That would never have happened to me alone.

You had to come here.

You had to have your own way.

Without taking me into consideration.

But you have always been that way.

Everything always centers on you.

You have never thought of me. Not you.

And no one else either.

Go away.

Why are you standing around here.

I don't want to be considerate of you anymore.

I have had to be considerate of you my whole life long.

Now I have some rights.

At least the right to be alone.

You egotist.

I hate you.

And how I hate you.

You have no idea how much I hate you.

Everything only for your sake.

Only for your sake."

Screaming words from a motionless face. As if her face held her body together.

The daughter went out of the room bent over. Went away and yet stayed quietly in the room. Stayed too long with her.

Hilde pours herself a second glass. Drinks it down in one gulp. Pours herself another one.

These sentence fragments from the kitchen. Why did I have to hear them. I have always managed not to hear so much. Why not these voices. Why of all things did I have to come here with her. Here to the beginningless end.

So I am still the daughter of Schalk.

So I am still one of the people from the house.

It doesn't exist. The time in between.

Anton never existed.

Only the house and the village existed.

And I have returned.

So my absence only served the purpose that I should come here again.

To come back here again and again.

So my other name was no protection.

So the house in the housing project was not stronger than the house outside the village.

So my love for Anton was only a limited love.

So the protection I got from Anton ended with his death.

So there is only me again and the house.

The house. The house. The house.

No house had colder walls

No house was so poorly soundproofed.

No house was darker.

No house was emptier.

No house was more stuffed full of people.

Out of no other house did there creep more despair.

I didn't forget this house in order to return. In order to die in this house. In order to be buried by these walls.

Time has stood still. In the village. In the house.

And only I believed that everything has changed.

I don't belong to the house anymore. Why didn't I die instead of Anton? Then I wouldn't have had to go into the house again.

Anton has LEFT ME ALONE.

As the house LEFT ME ALONE.

Even the daughter LEAVES me ALONE.

After she brought me back to the house.

The daughter I hate.

I have never asked anything of her.

Why did she bring me back to the house.

Isn't everything all the same to me now.

Now that I am back in the house.

She will have the story for her book after all.

What good was it, my silence.

My promise.

Anton broke his promise.

He had made it easy on himself.

He died.

Nothing holds me to my promise any longer.

He DESERTED me.

Left me in the house.

In this cold house that is smeared with blood.

But every house was bloody after all. There were bullet holes in every house. Dead bodies lay in every yard. My house was a house like every other house. And what right do they have to talk about my house. As if they did not come from similar houses themselves.

because the house is outside the village limits

because the village always gossiped about the house anyway

because there is more poverty in the house than in the village

because there is more drinking in the house

more beatings

more screaming

the village screams too and curses and drinks and beats and murders

The baker. Who had often not given us any bread. Even though the shelves were full. Hadn't he almost beaten his wife to death?

And the innkeeper. Who only gave credit to the villagers. Never to people from the house. Hadn't he drunk himself to death?

And the gawkers. The Sunday gawkers. The weekday gawkers. Who would stroll by the house. Why did they stare so. If only to see something terrible.

Only one person was honest. Anton. Only Anton didn't care that I came from a bleeding house. He was the only one, who admitted that his house bled also. Anton, who went with me into the housing project.

In order to leave the oozing houses behind us. Anton, who built a new house with me. Far away from the old house.

No longer an Anton. No longer a home.

Once more this house.

Once more together with the other people.

The other people.

They have continued living in February-houses.

Have never left the houses spattered with blood.

"Erika!

Damn it. Where are you!

To LEAVE me ALONE! That you can do.

That you were always able to do.

You. And all the others.

Sit down.

Sit in that chair there.

Don't look at me.

You shouldn't look at me.

Why are you trembling?

If someone has a reason to tremble, then it is I.

Am I trembling.

No.

Fetch me another bottle of wine.

No, two bottles.

Aren't you listening.

Fetch me more wine. Two bottles.

Quickly.

Otherwise I won't tell you anything.

Yes. Now you are going.

You'll do anything for your book.

Otherwise you would not condescend to do it.

A refined daughter. Who LETS her mother DOWN."

I have done everything for her. Everything. I did everything for Anton. Everything. They are ungrateful.

Egotistical.

I didn't raise her to be that way.

"Finally.

Where were you so long. All on account of these measly bottles.

She has been crying.

Don't be ridiculous.

No one cries here.

There will be no red eyelids.

Turn your head away.

I don't like weeping faces.

I was never allowed to cry.

Whenever I cried, I got five more whippings with the fly swatter."

Erika is sitting in the armchair with her back turned.

"Should I tell you now or not?" Erika gets up. Goes over to Hilde unsteadily. Whose hands are still lying clenched on the bedspread. She takes Hilde's hands.

Caresses them. Hilde doesn't feel touched. Only hears the words: "If you want, we can go home. Immediately."

No other sound in the room. Noise can be heard only from the village square. The prevailing stillness. In which Hilde thinks she hears the beating of her head. The wordless movement of her lips. Until she can finally scream.

"Go home! Go Home!

You are completely crazy!

There is no home for me anymore!

You took it away from me. You!

You are TO BLAME."

Hilde watches the daughter's face. The GUILT was not yet recognizable. But it wouldn't be long.

I only have to find the right words. The words which would lead to GUILT. The wine. Wine will help me. The wine will find the words for me. The words for that night and that day. The words for the preceding nights and the days thereafter will come of their own accord.

So it is true, what she once told me. That everything one experiences, encounters, simply everything is stored in our brain. No erasable tape is available to us. Other than a forgetting which is limited in time. Yes. Forgetting was something I was able to do. That had been a good, usable erasable tape. Even if Hannes had been skeptical about it.

Hannes. You didn't have an erasable tape. You envied me on account of my erasable tape.

Just as she will soon envy me on that account.

She, who brought me back to the house.

Into a night. Into a day.

Into a cold night. Into a cold day.

Into a February-night. Into a February-day.

Back to the beginning of my GUILT.

# 16

A scream awoke Hilde. A scream of which she didn't know, whether it came out of her or from outside. This had happened often lately.

There was a full moon. Breath remained visible for a long time in the room. Monika was still sleeping. Hilde felt the cold pearls of sweat on the nape of Monika's neck. She turned over carefully. Wanted to see her brothers. Wanted to see Hannes. Hannes and Walter lay on their backs. Sleeping. The bed beyond them was empty. Max and Stephen were sleeping over at the homes of friends.

Now she heard the loud sound again. It wasn't a scream. It was sirens. The sirens came from-there

— there —

—the concentration camp Mauthausen.

Don't you dare go over — there —. The threat of her parents. No official order had been necessary. In the house one sentence from Pesendorfer sufficed. No one had any business being — there —. Bent over, guilt-ridden heads.

— there — which was so near. — there — which was so visible.

Hilde now heard the shots.

Then the tenants of the house also woke up.

She heard a baby cry. And Mrs. Kals's voice. Which was supposed to lull the child to sleep. Pesendorfer must have opened the window. No one else would open the window. While the sirens were sounding. The sirens became louder. The father coughed in the next room. The mother repeated one sentence:

"Just stay in bed . . ."

Hilde became cold. She heard a motorcycle drive up from afar. Heard it stop in front of the house. The thick walls of the house didn't hold back the sounds of the motor. This sound!

It penetrated Hilde. Settled firmly in her bowels. Pesendorfer's footsteps echoed on the staircase.

Even at this late hour of the night he didn't forget his: "Heil Hitler."

Hilde didn't understand the words of the motorcyclist. Heard him drive away. Without taking the sound away out of her body. Heard then the order of Pesendorfer.

"Heil Hitler!

Everyone get up!

Immediately!

There will be a roll call in five minutes!"

Mrs. Wagner's voice: "Heil Hitler! What has happened?"
Pesendorfer's answer: That she'd learn soon enough.

The moon lit up Hannes's face. Made his soft face pale and
stern. Hilde got up. Awoke her brothers and her sister.

The mother came into the room. Shut the door with her
heavy body.

"If any of you don't want to go outside, you don't need
to.

I will say that you are sick."

All the while her eyes wandered from one son to the next.
Lingered on Monika.

Monika shook her head. Took Hilde's hand. Hilde pulled
her hand away. Hated the mother who only thought about
Monika. Hated the sister who wanted to make her shaking
hand strong by means of her own hand. She stood up next
to Hannes. Looked daringly at the mother.

The mother LOOKED PAST her.

"What do you think you'll be missing?

All right. Dress warmly. We can't know how long
Pesendorfer's roll call will last."

The father then came into the room. The family went out
as a unit. Uncommon solidarity. Which dissolved. When
they were outside.

Mrs. Emmerich came up to the mother. Talked insistently
to her. Hilde looked for Fritzi. Fritzi stood around freezing
and alone. Mrs. Wagner and Mr. Wagner paced back and
forth. The father shifted from one foot to the other. Even
now, when the moon light no longer lit up Hannes' face,
his face was pale. The sirens could still be heard from over
-there-. The barking of dogs. Now and then a motor
started to whine. They heard shooting. The people who
were waiting all winced at the same time. Pesendorfer
came. Demanded that they all get into a line. He called out
their names one at a time. Mrs. Kals was missing. Hilde's
mother wanted to get her.

No use.

The order forced her to remain standing in the line. Max
and Stephen's absence annoyed Pesendorfer.

It was typical of those two that they were not on hand
when Germany needed them for once.

Hilde felt a strange WARMTH in her, when she heard that
Germany NEEDED her tonight.

The great and mighty Germany.

Germany had to be very strong.

Stronger than anything else.

Germany could fetch her and all the tenants of the house out of bed in the middle of the night.

Germany, that was no longer just a word.

Germany, that was all of them.

That made them great and strong.

For the time being there was the great German moment of Pesendorfer. He divided up the house tenants. The mother had to watch the house with Mrs. Kals. Hilde and Monika were supposed to help them.

This great moment for Germany ended for Hilde with that. To help Germany. Separated from Hannes.

That made this Germany less significant for her. Took a lot of WARMTH out of her again. She stretched out her hand to Fritzi. Watched the mother and Monika all the while. Who clung to the mother. All the others were divided into two groups. In search troops. As Pesendorfer put it. He was in charge of one of them. The father had to take charge of the other one. He stood even more stiffly than usual in front of the tenants of the house. They were searching for — at this point Pesendorfer's voice became one of the voices which Hilde had heard up until then only on the radio:

"The most notorious criminals,

Russians

Russian convicts

murderers

thieves

killers

enemies

Russians, Russians, Rus . . .-"

His voice broke off, the voice, which was no longer a voice. Hannes stood shortly once again in the moon light. Hilde was afraid. She had to protect Hannes. Hannes, the ONLY brother among all the brothers. Hannes hid himself behind Walter. Then he slipped away. Pesendorfer was much too occupied with his wife. He didn't notice. Hilde saw how the mother made the sign of the cross. How Pesendorfer hit his wife. Who hung on him crying. Screamed at her: "A scandal! You of all people. You will regret it!" He pulled her into the house. The crowd of people heard how he locked the door behind her.

He came back. Ordered everyone to march on.

Shadows stayed in the yard.

Tree-shadows. People-shadows. Sound-shadows.

The mother thought they would do no more than freeze by staying there. They wouldn't be guarding anything.

"Let's go to the kitchen."

Hilde ran away. She had to look for Hannes. Only Hannes could drive away these shadows. Hannes whose slight body didn't leave a shadow.

It was suddenly quiet around her on the path with the apples trees. The sirens had stopped howling. Only the spotlights broke through the night. The stillness of the moon. The cold stillness. Then she heard a laughter that she had never heard before. Jubilation and terror was in it. It resembled the sirens.

She had to follow this laughter.

She sneaked up to the barn. From which it crept. Sneaked into the barn.

Saw how the blood spurted onto Pesendorfer.

Saw the hay fork in Mrs. Emmerich's hand.

Saw how she struck the hayfork against a shape lying on the ground. Against a shape like Hilde had never seen before. Against this bony face. Over which the skin was stretched.

Then she looked away.

Looked away as the hayfork stabbed at it.

Looked away from the other one who was lying under Pesendorfer's boot. Looked away from her brother Walter who stood leaning against the barn wall. Holding onto a fugitive whom he dared not let loose. Otherwise the fugitive would have collapsed. Hilde sensed how her

knees wanted to make her smaller, very small. But
something in her would not let her knees collapse. Held
onto the pictures. Held onto the big talk of Pesendorfer.
Tried to match the words to the pictures. To these helpless bodies.

Forbidden thoughts.

Hilde got a headache. She crept back to the path with the
apple trees. People were coming from the village. Armed
with threshers. With garden tools. They found fugitives in
the trees. They found people half dead in the snow.
Everywhere people found people.

Only Hilde was not found by anyone. She, who didn't
want anything more fervently than to be found. So that
there would be an end to it. To the forbidden thoughts.
To the GUILT. Of having betrayed Germany. To have to
continue betraying Germany. Because these pictures
remained. Because words could not banish them.

These bodies. Unarmed. Helpless. Frail.

At last two words sprang out of the shadows.

Two words stood clearly legible in the snow.

All words were tangible again on account of two vindicat-
ing words:

Forget it!

To repeat it in her thoughts. To utter it. To mutter it to
herself. To say it aloud. To shout it. To shout it to the
others. No other person was looking for words during this

February-night. The search of the others had nothing to do with her quest.

She went home with these two words.

Went into the house with these two words.

Went into her room with these words.

Hannes was there. Good old Hannes was there. Hannes, on whom she could lean.

But Hannes was no longer her Hannes. Hannes did not understand. Pushed her away. Pushed her back to her words. Gave her in addition two new words: "You too!"

Crying eyes. Trembling lips. Then he took her again into his arms. Laid her down on her bed. Covered her up. Hannes began to talk insistently to her. Quietly. He had hidden a fugitive in the wardrobe. No one had seen him. He was quite sure. Monika and Mrs. Kals were with the mother in the kitchen. The others were still on the manhunt.

That last word changed her face. Hilde was terrified. Hannes shook her again. Forced her to listen to him. She had to help him provide food for the fugitive. Bandages. The concealed person had a shot wound in the right upper arm. Hilde was supposed to help out in the infirmary. That way she could get hold of all the necessary things without being noticed.

When Hannes heard the two words, which Hilde wanted to give him, he became angry.

How could she be so dumb. She couldn't possibly believe that she would ever be able to forget this night. Or would she let herself be impressed by the talk of Pesendorfer.

"Everyone," he said then, "who doesn't do something against this manhunt makes himself GUILTY.

Are you listening. Everyone. Even you!"

Hannes let go of her. Took her hand. Lay down beside her. Hilde covered him up. They remained lying that way. Under one blanket. Until the father came back with the search troop. Then he got up. Joined this group unobtrusively. She stayed in bed. Was afraid. Concentrated her old fear onto the wardrobe. Onto this living wardrobe.

Tried to control her trembling body.

Tried to get up. To walk away from her fear. To go downstairs to Germany which was calling to her again. Calling loudly to her.

Calling so loudly as Hannes could never call to her.

Pesendorfer had returned with his group. Gave the order to line up. The line was formed. The roll call. It had proceeded satisfactorily. As he concluded. "because there are no casualties on the German side."

He announced the successful combat against "three Russian criminals."

He ordered the father to make his report. He stepped forward out of the line. Announced without looking up that they had not been able to capture anyone.

It had never been a matter of capture! How many Russian criminals had they been able to kill! That he wanted to know!

"And on the double!"

"None." The father announced. In a voice without shame. Or so Pesendorfer presented it.

"None," Mrs. Emmerich screamed.

"None," Walter also tried to scream.

But he only managed to say "no--" and stopped.

The others remained still.

Pesendorfer demanded an exact reporting. Father gave it. Told where they had searched. The others from his group nodded along assiduously. Hannes nodded the most vigorously of all. "A scandal. Such a scandal. A scandal for Germany," Pesendorfer screamed.

"A scandal for this German house."

And he had only remained living in this house, had scorned all the more attractive houses so that this German house would really become German.

"But such an incompetence is not permitted in Germany. Germany needs capable men and women. Not such nincompoops!"

When his voice began to break again, he let them go with a "Heil Hitler." Ordered them all to appear for roll call at 10 a.m.

The day was already at hand. The COLD had already penetrated her body. And the triumph had withdrawn from the eyes of those who had been successful.

Ashen faces. Behind which the ashen walls stood.

Shots even into the day.

The barking of dogs and morning church bells. The bells announced the Candlemas of the Mother Mary. In order to fill the church with blood.

To purify Mary.

How pure. How pure.

The pure Mary. The pure people. The pure village. The pure house.

Everything pure.

The tenants of the house got ready for church. Only the Pesendorfers never went to church. All the others went every Sunday. And on this day. For purification. Hannes did not want to go today. Hannes wanted to stay at home.

Hilde went along.

Silently. Struggling.

Caught between Germany and Hannes.

Germany or Hannes.

Germany or Hannes.

The WARMTH of Hannes or the WARMTH of Germany.

On the way home she decided for Germany.

Even the pastor had decided for Germany. Had encouraged them to continue the search. To search further. Until the last criminal had been found. Until this blemish had been washed away from the German earth. Until German soil had been purified again.

Whom should she tell it to?

Who was Germany?

Pesendorfer was out of the question.

She didn't want to help this Germany.

The father?

The father was already drunk again.

She couldn't trust a reeling Germany. She needed a firm German soil.

The mother? The mother, who always NEGLECTED her. Would she finally take a look at her?

Was the mother Germany?

Hadn't even Germany always NEGLECTED her? No further thoughts. She had made up her mind. She had decided in favor of Germany.

Therefore the mother.

The mother was walking further behind her. She moved slowly. Her fat body needed time. Hilde waited for her. Began to talk. At first stuttering. Then faster and faster. Watched the mother from the corner of her eyes. Whether she was really listening only to her. When she had finished, this woman looked at her as if Hilde were a stranger for her.

The mother said one sentence. One sentence, which the mother spoke only for her: "Are you not content that enough people have died?"

Then she dragged herself past Hilde into the house.

The mother was no longer Germany for her then. Germany was no longer a mother. There were only the tenants who were standing in a row. Hilde joined them.

A man of the Black Shirts from the village took over the father's group. They searched further.

The search at night. The search during the day. Searching. Searching.

The COLD remained.

Hilde did not dare go up to her room. Sat down in the stairwell.

Mrs. Kals sat next to her.

Then it became still in the house. It became stiller and stiller.

The echoing footsteps were to be heard when they had not yet entered the house. Echoed closer to the house. Echoed in the yard. Followed by a second pair of footsteps.

At first Hilde only saw the feet in the entrance way. Then she saw the uniform. Then it was Pesendorfer. Behind him a second uniform. Hilde remained sitting motionlessly. Next to her Mrs. Kals was trembling. The mother looked into the hall. Shut the door again, when she recognized those who had come in.

The boots stepped onto the stairs. Were in front of her face. Pushed her aside. Were behind her. Went up to the door of her room. Entered the room. Stopped in front of the wardrobe.

Now something flopped out of the wardrobe.

Now Pesendorfer laughed his laugh again. Now there was a dragging sound along with the sound of the boots.

Hilde saw the bundle being dragged. Mrs. Kals jumped up. Ran past the bundle to her baby.

They dragged the bundle past her. She looked at the
blood smeared, bony face of the bundle. The boots left
the house with the bundle. Remained near the bundle in
front of the house.

Silence.

Wanting to dance into this silence. To dance this silence
further. Only wanting to dance. Wanting to dance.

The mother came out of the kitchen. Looked up at her.
Hilde looked back. She did not know how they had been
able to find the bundle. She heard Mrs. Kals' crying. Her
baby's crying. Heard Mrs. Pesendorfer's question behind
her. "What's the matter now?"

Only perceived the disdain in her mother's face.

And Hannes? Where was Hannes? She had to warn
Hannes. She had to explain everything to him.

What should she explain to him?

The insecurity kept her on the stairwell.

Hannes and the father came home later with their group.
The bundle was still lying there beside the boots. They
waited until all the house tenants were back. Then
Pesendorfer ordered everyone to kick into the bundle.

But no foot stirred.

His boots kicked the bundle. Kicked. Until there was
nothing more for him to kick.

Lowered heads.

One after the other went into the house.

"Traitors of Germany!" screamed Pesendorfer after them.

"Traitors of Germany!"

Not one had raised his boot.

Not one.

Not one had trod on the boots of Pesendorfer.

Not one.

No foot stepped on the bundle.

Not one.

No foot stepped on Pesendorfer's boots.

Hilde went upstairs.

Heard Hannes come.

Crawled under her blanket.

When Hannes pulled the blanket away from her. She murmured:

"Forget it."

Hannes lay down on the bed opposite to hers.

Hilde crawled under her blanket again.

She would go to work in the infirmary tomorrow.

Hannes was picked up hours later by Pesendorfer. Hours later Hannes was brought back by Pesendorfer. Hilde went and got water and a towel. Washed blood off his face.

Hannes went to work the next morning just as he did every morning. Never went to work again.

No one had dared to wash away the blood from the house wall.

Monika took a tub of water and a scrub brush.

Scrubbed the house wall.

She got up for the last time to do that.

The sounds in the house the next morning were not different from those on previous days. Monika's sounds were missing. No one noticed the lack of her soft sounds.

The swastika flag was flying in the village.

When Hilde entered school, the words —

—the dead people—

were the main words of the day.

On her way to school she passed a mountain of dead people.

Two open trucks with dead people stood in the village.

The dead man from the house was in one of the trucks.

She did not recognize the bundle. Had only seen it as it was picked up. Many village houses were not yet washed clean. Many hands bore traces.

Her two words were taken up when the sentence—

—the Russians are coming—

had replaced the words—

—dead people—.

Then her two words became general usage for everyone for an indeterminate amount of time.

"Forget it."

# 17

Hilde heard the daughter toss and turn.

She should toss and turn. Why did she want to know everything. Why had she not accepted my two most important words.

I am tired.

Hilde wanted to sleep in her bed, in her house. Instead there was only this cold guest room for her. In which nothing was familiar to her. Besides the view of the window. The daughter had sat there previously. A table had stood there.

Have I forgotten anything?

She giggled.

I hope I have forgotten something. So that at least there remains one secret.

Sleep. Sleep.

Waiting for the shadows. Waiting for the February-shadows.

They have caught up with me. Too many shadows for me.

She awoke in the morning with a heavy head. The thunderstorm had become a continuous rain. The daughter is standing again in her place in front of the window. Her back is slouched.

That she can't stand up straight. But maybe it is better. When she turns her ugly face toward the floor. Hilde took a couple of headache pills. Washed them down with the rest of the acidulous wine.

"Let's leave at last!"

The daughter's eyes.

Shadow-eyes.

Hilde got up. Went into the shower on the corridor. She showered a long time. Made up her face in front of the mirror in the room.

Took her purse.

"Do you want breakfast?"

The daughter shook her head.

Sunday morning in the village.

All the village inhabitants had to go to church. That was good. Hilde did not want to be seen by anyone. Didn't want to see anyone. The strain of moving her face into friendliness. It would have been too much for her.

Hilde got into the driver's seat. The daughter didn't want her to drive. She had drunk too much yesterday. Hilde didn't pay any attention to her. The daughter stood indecisively. Slammed the door shut. Went to the other side.

"What are you going to do now."

"I don't know."

Hilde drove slowly out of the village. Speeded up on the country road. Clods of earth lay around. The tractor tires had let them lose.

"Don't drive so fast. It is slippery."

Hilde looked mockingly at the anxious daughter. Who still thought she knew everything better. Hilde stepped harder on the gas pedal.

Historical background

The so-called MÜHLVIERTLER HASENJAGD

(The Rabbit Hunt of the Mill District)

During the night preceding February 2, 1945 about 500 of the 570 prisoners of the special barracks number 20 broke out of the MAUTHAUSEN concentration camp. Mostly soviet officers were in this barracks. Seventeen survivors have been found. All the rest were murdered by the National Socialists and by the inhabitants of the Mill District, who had been "unpolitical" up until that time. Few of the Mill District dared come to anyone's aid.

The characters here are the invention of the author.

# AFTERWORD

Who is speaking here. A woman, Hilde. Right after the first sentences of the narrator her voice establishes itself. Whom does she address. Whose eyes observe her, who is really telling the story. What are the events which work their way out of her memory against her tenacious resistance. And why these chopped off, breathless sentences. The entire web of connections develops from them and from the pursuing questions and observations of the daughter, from which these sentences run away. Hilde, who was always ignored, lived in this web.

The book gripped my attention. The effort that it cost me to read it seemed necessary, not gratuitous. The structure of the text, which strives toward a disclosure, corresponds to the investigation, which the author undertook, and it corresponds also to the process of remembering. I had the feeling I was working along on an excavation project, the results of which terrified me. We participate in the convulsions of a woman who needs to cough up something terrible. A knowledge, a secret, which she almost does not recognize any longer, having shut it away so tightly within herself. "Forget it" were her words of survival, which camouflaged her even to her next of kin and drove her into an unholy self-forgetfulness. The book discloses this compulsion, incorruptibly but not mercilessly, because the daughter, who writes, who gets the secret out of her mother, is not guiltless and self-satisfied but rather a younger person who had it easier and better in life undeservedly and thanks to her mother. So that she could gather the knowledge and the strength, in order to ask questions.

Toward the end of the war, at the beginning of February, 1945, almost five hundred Soviet officers, who had fled the Mauthausen concentration camp, were mowed down by the inhabitants of the Mühlviertel in Upper Austria.

Elisabeth Reichart grew up in the Mühlviertel. Never, never did she hear even a single allusion concerning the mass murder from grown-ups, until she herself was almost grown-up. Then her grandmother spoke. We sat opposite one another in a restaurant in Vienna, when she told me about it, haltingly as she writes here. That this revelation should be the impetus for her first book is clear. And the shock which this revelation produced in her also had to find its way into this book.

But she had to try to understand nonetheless. She had to discover a person to understand, who was present and who was practically still a child. Who did not murder, but who could never speak. Simply pointing to guilt would have been easier, keeping herself out of the picture would have been easier. It was more difficult to track down the havoc which such circumstances wreak upon a person and yet to remain fair. More difficult to endure the ambivalent feelings, that engulf the narrator, while she discovers one layer after another not only in her protagonist but also in herself. Hatred and sympathy, horror and understanding, despair and guilt—all of which are also only to be detected from the reactions of the mother.

The author does not want to do to her protagonist what was done to her during her whole life. She does not want to make an object out of her. The long time she worked on this material, during which she was quite merciless toward herself, seems to me to have freed her from her blind anger and allowed her an insightful understanding that is more propitious for the future. By means of a double rupture, the author finds the possibility of freeing herself from the character in a conscientious, perhaps too conscientious fashion; the form, which appears strange, often strict and confined, can be set aside suddenly. When Hilde, the mother, who is apparently the center of concern the whole time, about whom this story is being written, suddenly breaks out of being a character and after she has read the manuscript of her daughter, intrudes in order to set matters right: I am not this woman. This is a figment of my daughter's imagination. She also never had a cat. Nothing but lies. Such a house never existed as little as did my drinking father.

Yet the house stands there and is difficult to forget. There is the drinking father. There is the village. To have placed all this there, as if out of stone, as if of flesh and blood and to characterize it at the same time as if it were an invention and to hold it in abeyance is the real artistic accomplishment of Elisabeth Reichart. That and the fact that she does not preach about a kind of human interaction which is different from the murderous kind she describes. Rather an attentiveness on the part of the author toward her character has found its way into the innermost structure of this book.

Drispeth, August, 1984                    Christa Wolf

# COMMENTARY

## Female Consciousness and the Holocaust

A key project of women writers today is to liberate female experience from its historically constructed prisons, the most powerful of which has been silence, the sheer unavailability of a narrative language. Elisabeth Reichart's *February Shadows* evokes the complexities of such silence through an intensive exploration of disturbed female experience. This short Austrian novel is an important contribution to the literature by and about women being created in our time—and particularly to that part of this literature which treats of mothers and daughters. Reichart's novel also operates significantly at the sociohistorical level. The relationship between the protagonist of the novel and her daughter is dramatized with reference to a little known but very revealing episode in the Nazi-Holocaust: the citizen murders of Russian soldiers that occurred near the concentration camp at Mauthausen in Austria on February 2, 1945. The fusion of the familial and the historical is viewed through the lens of postwar dislocation and rendered sayable through the compensatory power of the modernist literature of memory. Thus this first novel by a young Viennese woman unites three perspectives of interest to many readers of contemporary fiction: gender, memory and the totalitarian legacy.

The novel is, in one sense, the inner monologue of Hilde, who carries with her into old age the suffering she experienced as a child in a large, impoverished family in

Upper Austria. She learned self-effacement and silence as a means of dealing with the traumatic circumstances of this childhood. Her pain is now augmented by the death of her husband and by estrangement from her daughter, who is determined to write her mother's life story. Hilde had begun conversing largely with herself when her lines of communication with the outside world were disturbed, almost severed, after she witnessed as a child the Mauthausen killings. The novel is foremost a gradual unveiling of this bitter past, which Hilde tries to deny. The need to forget and the impulse to remember countermand one another throughout. If in one sense the novel is a monologue, in another it is a dialogue between mother and daughter. Blocks of resistance stand interspersed between breathless eruptions of the psyche, which build to a final discharge of emotionality when Hilde begins to speak to her daughter about the dreaded past. Although silence is at the center of *February Shadows*, suffering gradually finds its voice through the emergence of dialogue from the processes of writing.

The story narrated here points to the real depersonalization which women have traditionally experienced because of their radical lack of power and their impoverished interactions with the world. In this instance, Hilde's negative self-image is fashioned by the relations she has with the rest of her family while she is growing up. Her family lacks reciprocal affections and personal loyalty. Hilde's rootless and isolated consciousness in this family context is highlighted from various angles. The depersonalizing article "the" to designate her mother, father, and daughter, instead of the personal word "my," indicates the structural separation between Hilde's world and that of her family members. Elisabeth Reichart has stressed to me the importance of retaining this pronoun "the" even in the English translation as a way of indicating Hilde's estrangement from her family. Hilde's father, who was an alcoholic, controlled her life, without Hilde ever being able to understand the reasons for his behavior. He killed her pet cat and determined that she should not be allowed to continue school. "The" father is the family institution, which in its dynamics mirrors other institutions and other determinants of the social/historical world. The family here is not a bulwark against the state; rather the family as an institution prepares the child for political institutions by manipulating human desires ("Hilde felt a strange warmth within her, when she realized that Germany needed her tonight," p. 122). This institutional connection is made clear when Hilde asks: "Who was Germany?" "The father? The father was already drunk again. She couldn't trust a reeling Germany. She needed a firm German soil. The mother? The mother, who always neglected her . . . . She had made up her mind. She had decided in favor of Germany. Therefore the mother" (p. 131). Hilde is cheated of the emotional support and the ethical clarification which she might expect to find in a functional family. Thus she gives in to the norms of the society around her and becomes an agent of the Nazi state by betraying the fugitive whom her brother is hiding and bringing about her brother's death in the process. This is the decisive gap in her story ("I hope I have forgotten something. So at least there remains one secret," p. 139). And the memories of this deed fill the rest of her life with hatred, resentment and retribution.

The emotional emptiness remains in her life, even after Hilde escapes the confining circumstances of her childhood environment and the dreaded secret inscribed in it, by nabbing a husband with an academic degree and moving away from her hometown. Unlike her father, the man she marries is gentle and soft-spoken. Nonetheless, discontent smolders. If her husband would only look up just once from his newspaper and pay attention to her, then her world would be set right at last. The story suggests a confinement in her world which imposes itself on all changes, both real and imagined.

Reichart's novel addresses mother-daughter relations through the ways in which the two women in the novel both resist and support one another. The novel both shows why Hilde is silent and demonstrates the kind of intervention which gets her to speak. As a child Hilde was told to forget the Mauthausen incident; when she is an old woman, her daughter, Erika, prods her into remembering. Hilde has a stolid investment in her own victimization (that is all she knows; although she complains about it, she will not give it up). She also has intensely ambivalent feelings toward her own daughter, and resists the latter's efforts to pull her out of the labyrinth in which she is floundering. Hilde's inner monologue thus becomes also a dialogue with the daughter, who needs her mother's memory in order to make connections both personal and historical. The ostensible motivation for discovering such connections is the book that Erika is writing about her mother. The very act of writing such a book discloses the significance that Erika sees in her mother's life, and yet she herself is not prepared for all the horror it contains.

For Hilde perpetrated the pernicious patriarchical structure embodied in Hitler fascism through her own obedience, subordination, and self-hatred. This woman's identity is intertwined with the specific mentality of that time just as the mother-daughter relationship is also located in a specific social historical situation.

There has been a special emphasis on mother-daughter relations in recent works published by women since the 1970s. Works thus focused appeared first in the United States where the women's movement has set the pace for the rest of the world. Probably the most significant piece of nonfiction to appear there is Nancy Chodorow's social-psychological study of female bonding entitled *The Reproduction of Motherhood* (1978). Chodorow maintains that the experiences that women have in childhood, when establishing a sense of their own identity, are quite different from those of men. Chodorow theorizes that women form their identity in continuity with that of the mother rather than by disrupting it as men are thought to do during the preoedipal phase. Another approach to the topic of mothers and daughters has been to interrogate the connections between motherhood and Western patriarchical society. It is maintained, for instance, that mothers inadvertently reinforce male hegemony. Adrienne Rich's *Of Woman Born* (1976) articulates such a stance. Autobiographical works and oral history projects pursue this topic further. Nancy Friday's *My Mother Myself* (1977) is one such well-known autobiographical work.

Interview collections include Signe Hammer's *Daughters and Mothers: Mothers and Daughters* (1975) and Judith Arcana's *Our Mother's Daughters* (1979). Cathy Davidson and E. M. Broner broach the topic in the context of literary history in a collection of essays entitled: *The Lost Tradition: Mothers and Daughters in Literature* (1980). The investigation of mother daughter relations in German speaking countries has developed along similar lines. Karin Spielhofer discusses mother-daughter bonding in *Sanfte Ausbeutung* (Gentle Exploitation, 1985) while oral history projects include Erika Schilling's volume of interviews entitled: *Manchmal hasse ich meine Mutter* (Sometimes I Hate my Mother, 1981) and Jutta Menschik's *Ein Stück von mir: Mütter erzählen* (A Part Of Me: Mothers Talk, 1985).

Three fictional representations by Austrian and German women writers have a focus similar to that of Reichart's *February Shadows*: Elfriede Jelinek's *Die Klavierspielerin* (The Piano Player, 1983), Anna Mitgutsch's *Die Züchtigung* (Three Daughters, 1985), and Helga Novak's, *Die Eisheiligen* (The Ice Saints, 1979).

The number of cinematic texts about mothers and daughters directed by German filmmakers who are women stresses again how important this topic has become today: Helke Sanders, *Eine allseitig reduzierte Persönlichkeit* (A Personality Reduced on All Sides, 1977-78) Margarethe von Trotta, *Schwestern oder die Balance des Glücks* (Sisters or the Balance of Happiness, 1979), Jutta Brückner, *Hungerjahre—in einem reichen Land* (Hunger Years—in a Rich Land, 1979) and Helma Sanders-Brahms, *Deutschland, bleiche Mutter* (Germany, Pale Mother, 1980). Ingmar Bergman's film *Autumn Sonata* illustrates this mother-daughter focus in a cinematic text produced by a man. While Reichart transmits the consciousness of a mother, these writers depict primarily the perspectives of daughters who have been psychologically deformed by their relationship with their mothers. Like Hilde in Reichart's novel, Marie, the mother in Mitgutsch's *Three Daughters*, suffers severe emotional and physical neglect as a child. Like Hilde she also later escapes the confines of her childhood environment through marriage. But her daughter Vera is caught in the same vicious circle of emotional abuse. Vera similarly transmits her inability to form nourishing emotional attachments and her hatred and resentment on to her daughter:

> You only know you are unhappy; you press your fingernails into your flesh to convince yourself that pain is not the everyday form of existence; you pull back into yourself and few can reach you, and I look on helpless and ashamed. I did not succeed in breaking the chain. Here, too, I have remained my mother's daughter. [Anna Mitgutsch, *Three Daughters*, trans. Lisel Mueller (New York.: Harcourt Brace Jovanovich, 1987), 136.]

Psychological and physical pain are passed on through the generations as compensation for each generation's frustrations.

The violated self is an integral part of the violated world, and the particular events of Hilde's life enact a broader set of historical events, the second context in which the novel must be read. In fact, the novel has the specific diagnostic and cognitive function of clarifying what is arguably the single most disturbing fact of modern history, namely, the systematic extinction of human beings — the foundation of Hitler fascism. The central event in Hilde's remembered childhood is based on the so-called rabbit hunt of the Mill district when about five hundred prisoners, mostly Soviet officers, broke out of the concentration camp at Mauthausen. Most were tracked down and murdered by the civilians of the nearby village, who apparently wielded simple farm implements as weapons; the soldiers' frail, malnourished bodies offered little resistance to the pitchforks used to destroy them. The monologue leads to fundamental insights into the brutality of Hitler fascism as it was acted out, not by specially trained troops, but by ordinary people in small rural communities far from mainstream politics. Private memories function here to warn us about the underside of civilization.

Elisabeth Reichart does not directly tie this historical occurrence to the physical abuse and emotional deprivation that Hilde experiences. But the novel plays with the possible connections between the dehumanization in the world of a fictional character like Hilde and the real pathology inscribed in places like Mauthausen; the historical details woven into the narrative suggest these connections. Some of the historical references may pass unnoticed, but they are significant as context and should not be ignored: the public gathering mentioned in chapter two is a Nazi victory celebration; young women fulfilled the equivalent of military service by working one year on a farm, as Fritzi does, for instance, or in an office or factory; social outcasts live closer to the concentration camp than do respectable town dwellers (p. 112). The perspective here on the limited world and corrupt environment which transform individuals into mass murderers is circumspect, almost compassionate. But it does not mitigate the realities of inhumane behavior. For this text speaks also to the choice available to people whose lives seem to offer them few alternatives. Hilde's father refuses to participate actively in the manhunt, for instance. Hilde's brother, Hannes, articulates more clearly an ethical stance, when he says: "Everyone . . . who doesn't do something against this manhunt makes himself GUILTY" (p. 128). Hannes is hanged from the pear tree after his attempt to hide a fugitive is foiled. His is the only genuine resistance to the manhunt. There is but one consolation, the significance of which underpins the entire narration: the only way to a new beginning after the genocide sanctioned by Hitler fascism is through an interrogation of precisely this past.

The American novel, *Anya* (1974), by Susan Fromberg Schaeffer presents a foil to Elisabeth Reichart's novel in its weave of gender and historical issues. Schaeffer describes the fate of a highly assimilated Russian Jewish family living in Poland in the 1930s and the 1940s. She writes from the perspective of a single female consciousness, Anya Savikin, who grows up in a supportive family characterized by strong emotional attachments, caring, and personal loyalty. Through her close ties with her mother, she acquires the strategies to protect herself and her daughter during the siege of the Warsaw ghetto, her internment in the Kaiserwald concentration camp, and scavenging for a living at the close of the war. The significance of mother-daughter relations in these nego-tiations with the Holocaust is underscored by two inci-dents. It was a Nazi tactic to seek out the mothers of the children they intended to murder in order to murder them together. By holding up the abandoned children in the lineup of women, they used the children's recognition of

their mothers as a means of detecting these women. Anya
sabotages this practice by leaving her child to be adopted
by a Christian family. Anya's mother sabotages the tactic
further by hiding from Anya during the lineup and thus
ensuring Anya's survival. The powerful experiences of
being a mother and a daughter allow Anya to resist the
Holocaust itself, although the rest of her life, like that of
Hilde's in *February Shadows*, remains oppressed by the
unrelenting memory of the events of that time.

The intensely personal and sociohistorical content of
Reichart's novel is inescapably linguistic. Language func-
tions here to exteriorize the anguish, depression, and rage
of an older woman, Hilde, whose survival tactic is to be
silent about the privotal event in her life, the human
slaughter at Mauthausen, which gives rise to these emo-
tions. Avant-garde texts have an established pedigree in
twentieth century Austrian literature; one has only to
think of Franz Kafka, Ödön von Horváth, and Peter
Handke. The stylistic devices of this novel have affinities
to those deployed by Thomas Bernhard, who with his
some thirty works is the most widely discussed Austrian
writer today. The force with which this novel speaks both
to the specificity of women's experiences and to the
occurrence of genocide in our time has to do with the
central role played by its textuality. These cultural macro-
events are wholy encoded in the inherited narratives
which erupt into history; and their intensity can only be
regained through an analogous rupture of the realistic
conventions by which we shield ourselves from them.
Elisabeth Reichart articulates specific female and historical issues by means of idiosyncratic narrative devices that
aim to rupture the reader's expectations.

Reichart's gripping rendition of disturbed mental processes and guilt depends on the repetition of key images
and phrases (sometimes at widely spaced intervals), on
elliptical sentences and sentence fragments, and on
unusual punctuation and segmentation of sentences and
paragraphs. Consider, for example, Hilde's agitation
when she reads what her daughter has written about her:

> It is my life. Not her life. My life is no matter of
> concern for her. Of no concern. Why is she
> meddling in my life. I was never permitted to
> meddle in her life (p. 89).

Repetition conveys her consternation when she revisits
the scene of her youth, which is also the site of her guilt:

> So my absence only served the purpose that I
> should come here again.
>
> To come back here again and again.
>
> So my other name was no protection.
>
> So the house in the housing project was not
> stronger than the house outside the village.
>
> So my love for Anton was only a limited love.
>
> So the protection I got from Anton ended with his
> death.
>
> So there is only me again and the house.
>
> The house. The house. The house.

No house had colder walls.

No house was so poorly soundproofed.

No house was darker.

No house was emptier.

No house was more stuffed full of people.

Out of no other house did there creep more despair (p. 109-110).

No attempt is made to present Hilde's story in a sequential or expository fashion. Concrete descriptive details concerning her life are rare, but they are profoundly evocative. During the first meeting between Hilde's fiancé and her alcoholic father, for instance, Hilde focuses on how her father's drunken movements are passed on through the old large kitchen table to the other people sitting there (p. 33). The conformity of her hometown is expressed in this description of the people sitting in the local pub: "All the heads had turned toward them at the same time. The right hands took hold of the glasses. Took the glasses to the mouth. Put them back on the table firmly. All the heads turned away from them again. As if they had practiced this choral response" (p. 77). Another remark of Hilde suggests her orientation toward death and the retribution she believes awaits her: "Wherever I go, everywhere there are these wrinkled-up, old women waiting for me" (p. 103). And finally, the many questions without question marks are as cautious and tentative as all of Hilde's dealings with the world.

The style of Reichart's novel itself makes us painfully aware of whose story is being told; Hilde is a rigid, anxious person with a narrow perspective on the world. Reichart articulates this perspective by means of the associative sequences of Hilde's thought processes: her consciousness is alogical, obsessive and multi-directed. The sparse phraseology renders the hardening of her feelings and her denial of pain, and the stringent repetition evokes the sheer monotony of her existence, her fixations and her confusions. Much of her thinking takes place in truncated sentences. When she thinks about herself, she leaves off the pronoun "I." When she reads what her daughter has written about her, she denies its truth, so great is her selfloathing ("This woman, who is dealt with in broken-off sentences. I am not this woman," p. 88). To move beyond sentence fragments, to discover connections, would surely shatter the fragile sanity she has created for herself.

The images that surface in her mind demonstrate the associative and yet disjointed nature of consciousness at work. The cut on her leg which she gets from riding her bicycle, for instance, reminds her of her intolerance of the sight of blood (p. 48). When she worked as a nurse's aid in the hospital as a young girl, she was not bothered by blood (p. 88). When did she begin to fear the sight of blood, she asks herself. Only later in an entirely different context does she describe the house in which she was raised as a house from which blood oozes (p. 113). She is envious of the white pages of her daughter's world and the privileges these pages signify (p. 87) and yet these pages are precisely white and beyond her grasp. "She will suffocate in paper mountains" (p. 81), she says of her daughter.

The significance of the various images that surface within Hilde's consciousness, float a while, and then plunge out of sight, is beyond her understanding. But such failed awareness on the part of Hilde can be very revealing to the reader. Through figurations dispersed with apparent randomness throughout the narrative—the cat, Hilde's dancing, her father's tender hands, his fly swatter, the bundle and the barn— there emerges a commentary on the fickle distortion of memory in the context of contemporary history. The word "shadows," which occurs in the title and is frequently repeated in the novel, forms in the original Austrian text unusual word compounds. Its base meaning relates to the low ascent of the sun during February, which makes shadows more pronounced than in other seasons. In its extended sense the images of shadows in this novel call to mind the evil deeds that occurred in February and Hilde's guilty conscience, which connects personal history with communal ethics, however vaguely defined. This is a realm of shadow par excellence. The only time the word "shadows" is connected to someone other than Hilde occurs after Hilde tells Erika her tale of terror. Erika, haunted now too with an awareness of her mother's complicity, quickly acquires "shadow-eyes" (p. 140)

Elisabeth Reichart's narrative techniques signal the inadequacy of language and the indeterminacy of all knowledge to know, techniques frequently associated with the postmodern writing of authors such as Reichart's compatriot, Thomas Bernhard. Three of Bernhard's novels,

*Verstörung* (translated as *Gargoyles*), *Das Kalkwerk* (*The Lime Works*), and *Beton* (*Concrete*) deal with the problems of communicating memories in a sequential, expository fashion. Unlike Reichart's novel, these difficulties remain unresolved within the context of the novels themselves. Bernhard's long sentences evoke an associative, alogical stream of consciousness comparable to Reichart's. As an example, consider this sentence from Bernhard's novel *The Lime Works*:

> It was totally quiet when he, Konrad, was not working, when he was walking up and down, this way and that, turning things over in his mind, because when I am turning things over in my mind, he is supposed to have said, I am not actually working, i.e., of course I am working when I am thinking things over, but basically I do not really begin to do my work proper until after the phase of considerations and reconsiderations is ended, which is when I begin to do the actual work, but by then it's all likely to be all over with the quiet here, what with Hoeller starting to chop wood all of a sudden, or else the baker arrives, or the chimney sweep, or Stoerschneider turns up, or the man from the sawmill, or you arrive, Wieser arrives, Fro arrives, someone comes knocking at the door, or else my wife needs something or other. [Thomas Bernhard, *The Lime Works*, trans. Sophie Wilkins (Chicago: The University of Chicago Press, 1973)].

Bernhard's protagonists are as repetitious, contradictory and obsessed in their mental constructions as Elisabeth Reichart's Hilde.

The alienating scenario of Hilde's mind, and the profound negativity it inspires, might seem to place this prose in Bernhard's postmodern camp. But Reichart's novel is not self-subversive and hermetically closed in on itself, as is the case with the work of so many of her contemporaries. It builds a coherent story about a woman's self-definition and about a mother-daughter relationship and it makes a significant commentary on history out of the very processes by which it puts the story in question. The resonance of the word "shadows," for instance, creates a decisive interplay between Hilde's own internal drama and the social history underlying *February Shadows*. The text points beyond the novel to the world of its potential readers and, as such, is a profoundly feminist book. Elisabeth Reichart portrays women, in their silence as well as in their speaking, a world in which history and patriarchy have gone haywire. Hilde's deprived life is located at the center of a universal catastrophe; the radical negativity of such experience disturbs the bland surface of our world, a world that has abandoned its attempt to assimilate the meaning of a life like Hilde's. A world bent on forgetting needs "February Shadows."

Donna L. Hoffmeister